I0573751

No Secrets in Spandex

Toni Jones

CRIMSON
ROMANCE
Avon, Massachusetts

This edition published by
Crimson Romance
an imprint of F+W Media, Inc.
10151 Carver Road, Suite 200
Blue Ash, Ohio 45242

www.crimsonromance.com

ISBN 10: 1-4405-5995-3
ISBN 13: 978-1-4405-5995-2
eISBN 10: 1-4405-5996-1
eISBN 13: 978-1-4405-5996-9

Dedication

FOR CHELSEA, THE REDHEAD, AND FOR STEVEN, THE RACER.

Chapter One

When Ariel Hayes entered the lobby of the Alpenhof Hotel in Vail, Colorado, she stopped short. What was the word she was looking for? Oh, yeah.

Wow.

Her boss, Theo, might have economized on her plane ticket, but he'd made up for it in spades by putting her up in one of the most luxurious hotels she'd ever entered, let alone stayed in. *Of course,* thought Ariel wryly, *Theo hadn't had much of a choice.* If she was going to break a story on pro cyclist Jacob Hunter, they needed to stay at the same hotel. Things happened in the wee hours at hotel bars. Lounging in the Alpenhof would afford her priceless opportunities to catch Hunter with his guard down.

But when she'd heard "Alpenhof" she'd pictured a rustic chateau with cuckoo clocks. Maybe some wooden skis mounted over a little fireplace. Nothing in her experience had prepared her for *this.* An alpine palace. She hadn't realized that pro cyclists in training lived like princes.

A bellboy immediately relieved her of her suitcase and matching carry-on, and Ariel moved, in a daze, up to the marble-topped reception desk. Glancing around her as the pretty, trim woman behind the desk looked up her reservation, she tried not to gape at the grandeur of the lobby. At the bank of brass-doored elevators along the wall. At the plethora of blooming flower arrangements and the golden candelabra. At the sumptuously upholstered couches and armchairs arrayed around multiple fireplaces filled with cheerfully crackling flames.

Ariel felt self-conscious, gawking at the rich décor like she was still a country girl from a one-stoplight town, where the biggest building was the 4-H tent at the county fair. She'd worked hard to put that country girl far behind her. She recovered her poise and assumed the cool, slightly impatient expression that characterized the faces of her urban colleagues, most of them Manhattanites by birth. Theo always told her she was a very good actress, and it seemed he was right. The reservationist gave her a conciliatory smile.

"Thanks for your patience, Ms. Hayes," she said. "You're in the Trillium Suite, number six-twelve. The restaurant is on the second floor, and there's a bar on the eighth with beautiful views of the valley. You can order room service until midnight. The pool's on the roof—you've missed open hours for tonight, but for the remainder of your stay you'll be able to use it between eight a.m. and ten p.m. The gym on the floor below is open twenty-four hours. If you need anything at all, my name is Charlotte. I'll be happy to assist you in any way I can." Her smile widened.

Ariel was charmed by the sincerity, the openness, of the woman's smile. People were *friendlier* once you got outside city limits, she suddenly remembered, surprised that she'd forgotten. When was the last time she'd even left Manhattan? She'd covered a fairly dreadful story about a senior senator and a high school page in D.C. when she'd first been hired at *X-Ray Magazine* last spring. But muckraking on Capitol Hill didn't exactly afford her the opportunity to reacquaint herself with the friendliest, most sincere and open-hearted segments of the U.S. population.

Ariel couldn't help but beam back at the woman, her face lighting up as she let herself smile without a hint of urban reserve.

It felt good. It felt good to smile like that.

Maybe I'll like Colorado, she thought.

*

At first, she'd been resistant to every aspect of this assignment.

She had never heard of Jacob Hunter, had never thought twice about cycling (when she thought of bicycles the first image that sprang to her mind was her childhood neighbor, ancient Nancy Matthews, wobbling slowly up the street on a massively fendered Schwinn, the front basket holding a dozen eggs, the newspaper, and more often than not, Shirley, Nancy's club-footed Tabby . . . not exactly ESPN material) before Theo called her into his office the week before.

It was the end of the workday. Usually, she didn't mind putting in extra hours, particularly for the prospect of a juicy byline, but that Wednesday she'd been eager to get outside. By 5:45 she'd had it. She felt restless, claustrophobic. Maybe it was her rural upbringing. Maybe it was her early training as a dancer. But sometimes, after sitting all day in recycled air on the eighth floor of a skyscraper, she felt like she was going to explode. Like she needed to *run* out of the building, move her limbs, expand her lungs.

She knew what she was going to do. As she abandoned her cubicle, she was already anticipating her trajectory. First walk a block north to the fruit seller on the corner for a bag of plums and a bunch of grapes, then head west to the Hudson River. Walking alongside the Hudson, looking out at the solemn, dark ripples in the water, she always felt tranquil. So what if New Jersey hunkered unbeautifully on the other side of the river? In her mind, she could replace the dull buildings across the water with oak trees and the Coast Guard ships with summer swimmers. She could trace the Hudson north toward its source, through upstate New York, all the way to the sleepy town where she was raised. The Hudson River connected her hometown to the big city. It connected her with her past. With her father, whose ashes were sprinkled not far from one of this very river's gentle curves. The water she saw glistening beneath the George Washington Bridge had flowed through the fishing holes her father had taken her to as a girl.

Sometimes she still needed to feel close to him.

She was passing Theo's door when she heard his rich baritone, that unwelcome, cajoling note throbbing in his voice: "Do I hear the footfalls of my star reporter?"

She paused. Fatally. The plums and grapes, the long, leisurely stroll by the water, the tranquility . . . she saw it all vanish. Not today.

"You've got a minute, don't you? Come in here."

She sighed, her whole body slumping before she pulled herself together. Over the past year, she and Theo had developed a warm, easy, bantering friendship, but he was still her boss. She couldn't blow him off, citing her deep urge to commune with a river. That wasn't how the world worked.

"You're going to love it," Theo said as soon as she'd stepped into his office. Her heart sank as she glimpsed the tower of files on his desk.

"Hmmmm . . . " She raised an eyebrow. Theo's smiling, preemptive reassurance was triggering all of her alarms. He leaned back in his chair, tipping his head, fingertips pressed together, one of his favorite poses. He was definitely having his fun with her.

"It's wonderful," he said. "Pure Americana. The classic story of small town boy makes good. The stuff dreams are made of. Life affirming. Heartwarming."

Ariel snorted. She was still a fairly new hire, but she'd worked for *X-Ray Magazine* long enough to see through Theo's games—*X-Ray* was hardly known for its heartwarming stories. Ariel dropped into the room's other chair. *Patience,* she told herself. *The river isn't going anywhere. Sunset happens every day.*

I'll go tomorrow, she vowed. Then she wilted. At this rate, she had a lot of things to do "tomorrow." She tried not to review the mental list, but the items scrolled through her mind, little pleasures she kept putting off.

Walk by the river. Go to yoga. Take a bath. Cook a delicious meal. Read a book. Go to the Met. Run in Central Park. Make a dinner date with Jenna. Make a dinner date with a man . . . an intelligent, kind, attractive man willing to put up with her crazy schedule.

This man was out there. Jenna Pierce née Kain, her busy, successful, high-strung and now happily married college roommate, had assured her of this the last time they'd managed to find time to get together for a quick happy hour drink. Jenna had met her own husband, David, at a Yankees game and was now an indefatigable champion of serendipity, true love, and "getting yourself out there." Jenna just didn't understand that it wasn't so easy. Ariel wasn't being stubborn, as Jenna often exclaimed in disgust. It wasn't that she didn't *want* to meet the man of her dreams. It was just that she needed to invest so much time and energy into building her name as a journalist that other activities—like parking herself in areas with a high level of foot traffic of eligible bachelors—fell by the wayside. She didn't have time to make a rendezvous with destiny. She would have to worry about finding Mr. Right . . . tomorrow.

Tomorrow. When Little Orphan Annie said it, it sounded so hopeful. For a woman inching toward her thirties, it had the ring of doom.

Theo paid no attention to Ariel's pained expression. He was gloating. With unconcealed relish, he handed her a glossy 8 x 10. A publicity shot. A blond man distractingly encased in skin-tight cycling gear, standing in front of a bike with a look of predatory arrogance on his handsome face. Theo tapped the photo significantly, and Ariel almost expected him to say, "Behold!"

She looked at the blond man, his taut body, his insanely snug outfit leaving nothing to the imagination. "He *is* heartwarming," she said.

"Jacob Hunter," said Theo almost reverently, hamming it up.

Ariel let the silence stretch out. Jacob Hunter. Not ringing any bells. "Nope," she said finally. "Never heard of him."

Theo rifled through his stack of files and flipped open a *Vogue*. "But you've *seen* him before?" he asked. "Yes? Think hard."

The golden-eyed, impossibly chiseled spokesman for the new Emanuel Ungaro sunglasses line—some of the most expensive men's eyewear on the market. Who hadn't seen him? He was pasted on twenty-foot high billboards in Times Square.

Oh hell, thought Ariel.

"I think he was on the side of the bus I took to work today," she said. She examined the publicity shot and the *Vogue* ad, glancing back and forth between the two. In the ad, he wore the same look of cocksure challenge, as if he expected to dominate anyone who strayed into his path. The same razor-cut swath of straw blond hair swept over his forehead, hanging over his left eye. The power of his stare was in no way mitigated by this partial concealment. Jacob Hunter looked like he could and would crush anything—or anyone—who opposed him.

"Feeling fluttery?" Theo grinned and Ariel batted him with the *Vogue*.

"Is this where we bond over our taste in boys?" she said dryly. Theo was always trying to tease and goad, and he flirted with her outrageously. His being in a fulfilling, committed, long-term relationship with a handsome orthodontist named Richard helped him to get away with it.

"Of course not," he rolled his eyes. "I have a much darker agenda. Listen. Jacob Hunter grew up in nowhere, Colorado. Every day, he rode his bike up and down abandoned gold rush wagon roads, until he got up the nerve to enter his first race at nineteen. Suddenly, he's the hottest pro cyclist in the world. It's a fairytale story."

"Doesn't sound too dark," commented Ariel skeptically.

"Fairy tales are always dark," said Theo. "Also, you can't believe them. Jacob Hunter is no Disney prince."

"What's the angle?" asked Ariel cautiously and Theo leveled his eyes at her.

"Last year, Jacob Hunter came out of nowhere to upset the top European racers," said Theo. "He's so fast, so good . . . "

"He's *too* good," finished Ariel, getting into the spirit of things. "Too good to be true."

"Rumor has it the small town hero is getting help," said Theo.

"Performance enhancing drugs?" asked Ariel.

Theo nodded. "It's a major issue in professional sports. Maybe *the* major issue. *X-Ray* has never run a sports story, but, really, sports have never been more controversial. Breaking a story on Jacob Hunter will give us the perfect opportunity to reach a broader audience . . ."

"While at the same time exposing a social problem that can serve as an indicator of our nation's attitude toward health," said Ariel dutifully. Theo *loved* to take the nation's pulse. If he didn't talk so much about men and wine, she'd worry it was his favorite thing. He gave her a mock glare.

"Am I that predictable?" he asked.

"No." Ariel sighed. "I'm just that well-trained." And she'd gone straight home—no river—to begin her research on Jacob Hunter.

Before she knew it she was on the plane to Colorado. It hadn't seemed real until the nose of the plane lifted and the wheels left the ground. She'd looked out the window and seen the borough of Queens spread out beneath her, rows and rows of houses shining dimly through the gray mist. She'd seen the grid of city streets, crosscut by expressways and parkways, millions of cars and cabs and buses and delivery vans racing over them. After a while, there'd been nothing to see. Only empty air all around, empty air grading into white distance.

Now she was here, pleasantly surprised by the Alpenhoff. Ready for a challenge. *Excited* for a challenge.

I might as well as enjoy this trip, she thought as she headed to her room. Maybe the mountain air and the friendly people would work wonders. As for the assignment itself . . . well, that might be fun, too. Given what she'd learned so far about unpredictable, violent, and impossibly arrogant Jacob Hunter, taking him down had begun to seem very enjoyable indeed.

Chapter Two

The Trillium suite fulfilled all the promises of the lobby below. It was gracious. Expansive. Tastefully decorated. The tub was larger than the entire bathroom of her meager Manhattan apartment, and the bed was bigger than her kitchen. She sat down on a loveseat, trying to collect her thoughts. Theo had been in touch with Jacob Hunter's sponsors and had arranged an interview for noon the next day. A few hours later, Hunter would be competing in an exhibition criterium for the Colorado Classic.

Ariel opened her tidy binder of Jacob Hunter related photos and articles and reread an article describing the race. The Colorado Classic was brand new and promised to be the most grueling race on the circuit.

Competitors were to ride well over a hundred miles through stupendously mountainous terrain. They would have to endure extreme temperature fluctuations. Thinning air. Road surfaces that ranged from rutted pavement to gravel. Snow squalls could happen at any moment in Colorado, even in the summer—white outs that made it impossible to see the curves of the winding roads.

Ariel shuddered. *White outs.* She didn't want to think about the kinds of accidents that could happen in unexpected blizzards. She flipped forward in the binder and looked again at pages torn from an upscale men's magazine. The pages displayed an artfully staged photo spread by a prominent photographer. Jacob appeared in a sumptuous luxury suite surrounded by attentive models— impossibly leggy women with the kind of bone structure Ariel had always wished for and never had a chance of attaining. In one photograph, Jacob lounged in a Jacuzzi. He looked bored, martini in hand, staring into space while the girls lathered and shaved the tanned, incredibly muscular leg he'd thrown over the side of the tub.

When Ariel had first noticed that particular shot, she'd taken the magazine straight to Theo. "Theo," she said. "Help."

Theo laughed. "Cyclists shave," he said. "It helps when they crash and mangle their legs on the pavement."

Of course.

"Why aren't you doing this piece," she'd muttered, "since you actually know something about competitive cycling?" She leaned over and dug a handful of raisins and pumpkin seeds out of the bag of organic trail mix on his desk. Theo leaned back in his chair, watching her resentful munching with an expression of amused complacency.

"*Why* you know something about competitive cycling is a mystery to me," Ariel continued, swallowing. Her fit of pique was already subsiding, but she could tell from Theo's indulgent posture that he was enjoying her complaints. She took another handful of trail mix, pouting. "Watching someone ride a bike is about as interesting as watching paint dry," she said, dropping into a chair.

Theo was watching her, delighted.

Sadist, she thought, her grumpiness tinged with affection.

"I love it when you get all gingery." Theo pressed his fingertips together. "And there is *nothing* I like more than watching a wet chartreuse lighten over several hours to a summery dry lawn green on a bedroom wall."

He laughed at Ariel's outrage.

"Eat some more nuts," he said, reaching out and giving the bag a shove. "Your blood sugar seems a little low. I gave *you* the assignment for many reasons. I know a thing or two about sports, but *you* are an athlete. And while I am a lovely man, you are a lovely woman, and Jacob Hunter is known to be susceptible to the second category. Otherwise I'd give it a shot."

"The assignment?" asked Ariel.

"All of it," said Theo coyly.

That was enough to shut her up.

To call her an athlete . . . Ariel appreciated Theo's compliment, but she was fairly sure Jacob Hunter—and all of the other sweaty, over-muscled, testosterone-addled men she'd be dealing with—wouldn't see it that way. Ariel was, or had been, a classically trained ballerina. She'd gone from dance recitals in a small, upstate town to the mirrored studios of Julliard, dreaming of debuting onstage at Lincoln Center as Odette in Swan Lake. Once, that dream had seemed within her grasp. She was remarkably talented; more importantly, she'd given her whole life to dance.

Her father, an English teacher, had cautioned her to hold a little back, to develop other skills, to have a backup plan, but she'd had a hard time following his advice. Although she never felt that she fit well socially within the culture of ballet, among the stick-thin, swan-necked blond girls with their perfect buns and perfect turn-out, she lived and breathed the spirit of dance. And eventually she found herself rising above those pretty blond heads, soloing out in the footlights while the girls who'd mocked her voluptuous figure and uncontrollable red hair stayed in the chorus.

A foot injury in her second year at Julliard put an end to all her dreams. A tiny bone—something she'd never heard of and couldn't pronounce—broke under the impact of a grand jeté she'd landed just slightly wrong. The bone wasn't something that could be splinted; she'd had to stay off her feet—how hard that was to do she'd never imagined until she tried it for four months—to let it heal on its own. When she finally went back to classes, not only had she lost the conditioning she'd worked so hard to achieve, it was immediately clear that however well her foot might hold up in her everyday life, it was no longer able to take the stresses of a serious dance career. By the end of each three-hour master class, she was sobbing, half in pain, half in frustration.

It was only months later, after she'd mourned her lost future, that she began to remember, and appreciate, her father's advice. She enrolled at NYU as an English major, then switched to journalism. She'd discovered—to her surprise—that her life was big enough for two passions. She loved everything about it—the sleuth-work of research, scrambling for deadlines, exposure to the most captivating personalities and burning issues of the times.

Not that she didn't have regrets. Not that she didn't miss pushing her body to the limit . . . the almost unbearable rigor and the giddy reward. She couldn't bear to dance even casually anymore, to feel the results of her lack of regular practice, her clumsiness. After spending years learning to fly through the air, she was earthbound, wings clipped. She hated to be reminded.

And now she'd turned sports reporter overnight.

"This is the plan," Theo had told her. "As far as anyone knows, you're a reporter with *Cycling Today*. You're in Colorado to watch Jacob train and race, but also to learn a thing or two about the man behind the cyclist. It's a fluff article. A celebrity profile."

"A fluff article," grumbled Ariel.

"It'll give you license to giggle," said Theo. "To bat your eyes." At Ariel's furious expression, Theo laughed aloud. He aimed a blow at Ariel's mass of unruly red curls with a rolled up copy of *Dwell*.

"I didn't become a journalist to bat my eyes," said Ariel stiffly. Theo shook his head.

"Why *did* I give you this assignment?" He shot her a mournful look. "The opportunity to go undercover among the hard-bodies is completely wasted on you. Listen, just pretend you're having fun. Pretend you're a fan. Soften him up, get him to relax, and bam! Get the goods. You can think of this as your own little Temperance crusade. An assault on the unbridled male egotism of the sports world. Remember how much discipline and hard work it takes to be a ballerina? And how the media doesn't pay a lick of attention? Think of all the dedicated athletes that never get any respect, let alone a shoe franchise. Too many big men in the limelight owe it all to a little pill. Get them out of the way and there's more room for everyone else. For the *real* He-Men." He grinned. "And She-Men."

"She-Women?" questioned Ariel delicately.

"Whatever," said Theo. "Now go get him. Oh, and Ariel . . . "

"Yes?" she said.

"While you're out there *pretending* to have fun . . . "

She arched a brow.

"Try to have a little fun, okay? It won't kill you."

"Thanks, Theo."

"Anytime."

Scrutinizing another photograph of Jacob Hunter, this time repping a cycling shoe, Ariel heard Theo's words echo in her head.

Too many big men owe it all to a little pill.

Did that body come from a bottle? She gnawed her lower lip, peering at the photo as though it would divulge Jacob Hunter's secrets.

The man was broad shouldered and lean; his upper body was classically proportioned, tanned to the color of tawny honey, while his legs were massively developed, like anatomy diagrams that showed each separate muscle in perfect definition, covered in smooth, golden skin that shone and rippled with the curves of the underlying shapes. Unbidden, the image of a racehorse's glossy flank sprang into Ariel's mind. She caught her breath. The muscles in her inner thighs were tightening.

God, what this man could do from a photograph . . . what would it be like when she was presented with Jacob Hunter in the flesh?

She flopped back on the enormous bed, rubbed her temples. Lucky for her, he would probably become a whole lot more resistible once she got into proximity to his massive ego.

Focus, Ariel. She sat up on the bed, leaned over the edge, and retrieved her notebook from her bag. She had work to do. An interview to prepare. What could she possibly ask Jacob Hunter? Her mind was as blank as the paper.

Do Italian models really shave your legs? Ariel groaned and threw herself back down on the bed. The smoothness of the fabric sent a shiver through her body. She imagined sliding her hands up another smooth, taut surface . . . .

What do a pro cyclist's legs feel like?

Ariel sat up quickly. She raked a hand through her hair and straightened her shoulders. Even a fluff journalist should have better questions than the ones she'd been coming up with! She paced the thick carpet. *Small town hero. Home grown Colorado.* Ariel sat down again and took up the pen with a determined air. She scribbled a line.

"How does it feel to be racing in your home state after so many successes in Europe?"

Not bad, she thought.

"You're the favorite going into this race. Will victory on Colorado soil be sweeter?"

She sighed. This wasn't exactly the incisive, hard-nosed interrogatory technique she'd cultivated in her journalistic career to date. But, she reasoned, she'd have to put him at ease first if she wanted him to believe that she was a glorified gossip columnist for a sympathetic publication.

Giving the list of questions up for a time when she felt more mentally astute, she began to flip through the issues of *Cycling Today* she'd bought before leaving New York, underlining the terms she'd have to look up. Peloton? Breakaway? Embrocation? She sighed. She had a lot of homework to do if she was going to convince anyone, let alone a professional cyclist, his trainer, and teammates, that she had anything to do with this particular specialty publication.

On the bedside table, several local newspapers were neatly stacked. Each one featured a front-page story about the next day's qualifying race. It was clearly a tourist attraction. It was also clear that Jacob Hunter was the main event. She began to page through the papers. Once she got past the cover stories, she found the same kinds of local-interest articles, petty editorials, want ads, and crime blotters she'd expect from small papers anywhere. Small-time politicians bickering with the school board. Bored teenagers vandalizing cars and buildings downtown.

To an outsider, Vail was all glitz and glamour, but she could already see through the façade to the underlying dynamics. Vail depended on tourism, and the people in the surrounding areas—small towns with limited options—depended on Vail for their livelihoods. Ariel herself came from dairy country, but she'd had friends from farther upstate and from Vermont whose towns depended on seasonal attractions. Autumn foliage. Skiing. She had a sense of how the tourist economy worked. And a sense of the resentments it raised.

An article on the second page of the third paper she looked at—a seedier looking rag than the other two—caught her eye immediately. The headline read: "Hunter incites barroom brawl, narrowly avoids arrest."

Ariel felt her pulse quicken. The article described an event that had taken place over the past weekend in the neighboring town of Minturn, Colorado. The prose was sensational, and took not a few liberties with grammar, but Ariel gathered that the story boiled down to this: Jacob Hunter had been involved in what was described as a "heated verbal exchange" with someone identified as "Brian Jenks, area man." Ariel jotted down the name excitedly. Their verbal exchange had quickly progressed to an exchange of blows. Despite the headline, it apparently wasn't clear which of the men had thrown the first punch—the only thing that saved one or the other from being arrested and charged with assault and battery. Neither of the men would disclose the nature of their disagreement, and none of the witnesses questioned had heard anything that shed any light on the issue.

Ariel's journalistic spider-sense was tingling. Was Jacob's fight a result of "'roid rage?" She'd learned that cyclists rarely used actual steroids. They didn't want to gain the bulk. A boxy physique would interfere with their ability to haul themselves and their bicycles up mountainsides as fast as possible. But testosterone was frequently increased by artificial means, and testosterone could certainly drive what started out as typical male energy into the terrain of frightening, hair-trigger aggression.

Some small town hero, thought Ariel. *How does it feel to be a thuggish fraud?*

Ariel put down the paper and leaned back on the couch. Her diligence had paid off. She felt satisfied. Hunter's bar fight hadn't made national news. With any luck, it wouldn't. That is, not until she found Brian Jenks and got the real story for an *X-Ray* exclusive.

The satisfaction was soon replaced by fatigue. But beneath the fatigue, she could sense a humming tension. Her muscles felt shaky. Over-caffeinated. Under-used. She already knew she wouldn't be able to sleep.

A walk, she thought. She slipped her room key into her pocket and opened the door. The plush corridor was completely empty, and she padded silently through the maze of hallways. Armchairs were arranged in sitting areas by the elevators, and she paused here and there to inspect piles of magazines on low tables. They all had to do with cycling. Skiing. Fishing.

Coloradans love their sports, thought Ariel.

She took the elevator down to the lobby. The friendly woman at the reception desk had been replaced by a young man. The look he gave Ariel was more than friendly.

She flushed at the unexpected male appraisal. Surely she didn't warrant that appreciative expression. Not in her casual, rumpled travel clothes, jeans and a boat-necked blue tee.

It was midnight. A few hotel guests were sitting around the fire with martini glasses talking quietly. The young man was just bored.

Ariel wound her way back to the elevators. She pressed the button for her floor—then, as the elevator glided upwards, leaned forward impulsively. She hit the button for the roof.

Chapter Three

The elevator door opened onto a scene of celestial splendor. During the day, she was sure the rooftop would boast an unparalleled view of the valley and the surrounding mountain peaks. But the vast bowl of absolutely black sky spangled with more stars than Ariel had ever seen far surpassed the glory of the daytime landscape.

She walked cautiously onto the cool marble that surrounded the swimming pool. The pool was large, the water dark, reflecting a thousand twinkling stars in its still surface. Ariel slipped off her sandals. She dipped a toe into the water. It was mild, almost warm. The night air was deliciously cool. Still. Silent. She felt hot and sticky from her travels. A wild impulse bloomed within her.

Suddenly, she was almost laughing. The air was so pure. The stars were so close. She felt the tension leaving her body. This was worth missing a few strolls by the Hudson. This was paradise.

She looked around, but of course there was no one. It was late. Anyone awake in Vail was out and about, drinking, mingling. She'd found a private spot. She was alone on the roof of the world.

Giddy, she stripped drown to her lace panties and bra and stood for a moment, face tipped up to the stars. She held up her arms in fourth position, turned a double pirouette. What had come over her? Was it the altitude? She didn't care. Without another thought, she glissaded to the edge of the pool.

Diving into the water felt like falling into the sky itself . . .

Instantly refreshed, she set herself to swimming laps, making up for the forced inactivity of her day of cabs and planes, hours and hours in transit. She hated days when she didn't move her body; going without any exercise left her jittery and off-balance. When she had counted off twenty laps, she let herself float like a leaf on the surface of the water, gazing up into the jeweled night. Suddenly, a shiver ran through her body. She heard nothing, saw nothing, but she knew she was no longer alone.

A splash in the water near her sent a surge of adrenaline rocketing through her veins. She felt something stroke her leg as a body moved past her underwater. She began to count in her head. One one-thousand. Two one-thousand. Three one-thousand. She kept counting. Didn't whoever it was need to breathe?

A head surfaced, mere feet from where she was treading water, but it too dark to see the person clearly. Before she could do anything, a husky baritone came out of the darkness. The man who spoke didn't sound remotely winded.

"The pool's closed for the night," he said. The observation was so preposterous that Ariel almost laughed aloud in spite of herself.

"Are you the hotel security guard?" she said.

"Would you believe lifeguard?" Ariel could tell from the man's voice that he was smiling.

"Aren't you off duty at this hour?" she responded.

Her alarm at finding her idyll interrupted by a strange man was swiftly transforming into a wild gaiety. A feeling of exhilaration. It was the night sky, the soft caress of the water, the distance from all the clutter and noise of New York City. She felt daring, free, invincible. She heard her own voice as though she were floating above her body. She sounded relaxed and flirtatious. She never sounded like that. Her voice usually had a pinched quality. Guarded. Even harsh. Theo had once called it a "go-thither" voice.

The man swam closer. Ariel could see the silhouette of muscled arms stroking the water.

"I take my job seriously," the man said. "A good lifeguard is never off duty. Not when there are people in the water."

"I take my job seriously, too," said Ariel. She felt her heel bump the side of the pool and realized she'd been drifting backwards, away from the man.

"But you're willing to break the rules," said the teasing baritone.

"What do you mean?" said Ariel.

"Well . . . " The man closed the distance between them. Ariel felt his hard, slippery arm brush her shoulder as he reached out to put a hand on the marble. "The pool's closed," he said.

"Here we are again." Ariel laughed, painfully aware of the nearness of his body. His legs scissored the water to keep him afloat. She felt his thigh brush hers.

"Two rule-breakers," he whispered.

Ariel strained her eyes but she still couldn't make out his features. Only the dark outline of his broad shoulders, the line of his throat.

"I wanted to come to the roof," she said. "I live in a city. I don't think I've seen the stars in years."

He lifted a dripping arm and pointed. She tried to look at the sky and not the unbelievably sexy contours of his bicep.

For the second time that night, Ariel struggled for the right word. *Wow.*

She might not be able to see his face, but she could see enough to know that this man had a stunning body. Maybe he *was* a lifeguard.

"The big dipper," he was saying. "Follow the line through the two stars that form the bottom of the bowl. That's Polaris."

"Polaris," she repeated. She could feel him look at her.

"The North Star," he said. He was so close she could feel his warm breath. "The pole star. It guides nomads. Wanderers."

Ariel's breath came shallowly. She'd never felt so drawn to another person. The sound of his voice. The heat of his body.

I can't even see his face, she told herself. *I don't know his name. This is crazy.* But she couldn't deny it. Her whole body responded to him. His presence was teasing, gentle. Overwhelmingly, frighteningly male.

She heard herself asking: "Are you a wanderer?"

"Sometimes," he whispered. He slid forward through the water, bracing himself against marble edge of the pool, arms on either side of her. She was trapped. She couldn't move. Couldn't breathe.

"Tonight I seem to have been guided to you . . . "

And with that, his lips lowered onto hers.

His kiss rocked her to her core. Desire bloomed low in her belly and rippled out like an earthquake, until even her fingertips felt hot, achy, super-sensitive. She could feel her pulse quicken, hear the blood pounding in her ears. She slid down into the water and he gripped her against his chest, his powerful legs keeping both their heads above water. His hands moved up her back, buried themselves in her wet locks. His tongue moved against hers. Hot. Expert. Insistent. She moaned and he deepened the kiss. They sank into the water, entwined, and surfaced, sputtering and laughing.

"Some lifeguard," she said, her voice rich and low with desire. She took a steadying breath and put an arm behind her to brace herself on the edge of the pool. In a millisecond, he was upon her, his swift movement through the water sending a delicious wave that slapped against her breasts and made her gasp.

She felt one of his hard thighs nestle between her legs. Before she could stop herself, she ran her fingertips over the rock-hard muscles of his impressively wide chest. She let her fingertips drift up the column of his throat, play along the strong jaw.

She needed to feel him, know him.

She touched his lips and felt them part. Sharp teeth caught her fingertip in a playful bite.

What she was doing? Fondling a stranger in a pool at midnight . . . Something more than just the altitude was to blame. Ariel was never this uninhibited with guys. Maybe . . . maybe she was afraid. Afraid of loving and losing . . . of being left even lonelier than she already was . . . She had already lost so much.

Well, she wasn't acting afraid tonight.

The man let his knuckles graze her lips. He dropped his hand to her clavicle, then slid a finger down to the tops of her breasts.

She held her breath as his fingers slid deeper, inside the scrap of damp lace that hid her painfully erect nipples.

Hid her nipples? What she was thinking? Neither of them could see anything. It was pitch black. It was madness.

What was he wearing? His thigh shifted and she felt the answer to her question. Nothing. He was wearing nothing. She felt the shocking length of his arousal, hot and hard, pressing against her.

"You're beautiful," he said hoarsely.

With a smooth, athletic motion, she pulled herself from the water and stood dripping on the marble. Suddenly, he stood beside her, water cascading from muscles that seemed to shine with dark light.

"How can you tell?" she asked breathlessly.

He didn't answer. He simply pulled her toward him, molded her body to his. His hands encircled the narrowness of her waist, cupped her buttocks. She felt a different kind of moisture gathering between her legs. A heaviness. A driving need. *Oh God.* She surrendered to his kiss, opening her mouth to allow him deeper access. Melting into him. Forgetting everything but the sensations he sent coursing through her.

All those years of toning her muscles. Conditioning herself. Making her body the perfect instrument. An instrument that nobody had played. Really played. Made sing.

Ariel quivered on the rooftop, every nerve fiber vibrating. What had she been missing? What was she doing? It was too much. Too fast.

Exerting a tremendous amount of self-control, she pulled away.

"I'm not a one-night-stand kind of girl," she whispered, hearing the raw quiver in her voice, the lack of conviction—a lack of conviction that had never been there before.

"Fair enough" the man said gently. He stepped back. As soon as his body no longer touched hers, Ariel was suddenly cold. She shivered and wrapped her arms around herself. She felt desolate—

wanting and not wanting him to push beyond her words to the truth of what she was feeling, to challenge her. Her objections could be so easily overturned.

Before she had a chance to do something crazy—throw herself back into his arms, renew their kiss—the man reached out, stroked her cheek for a fleeting instant, then turned. He murmured, "Goodnight," over his shoulder as he walked away, then disappeared through the door leading to the stairwell. He was silhouetted for a moment in the light from within. Ariel saw that he'd wrapped a towel around his waist, but she still couldn't see his face. The word *goodnight* echoed in Ariel's ears. What had she heard in his voice? She wondered if he was as shaken as she was by what had just happened. Ariel knew she'd be hearing that word throb in her mind for a very long time.

Goodnight. She'd never realized it could sound so sexy.

Why was she even now thinking of how it might have felt to continue that kiss, to run her hands down his back, to be pressed into the tiled surface of the rooftop under his weight, to see the stars glimmering over his shoulder?

Ariel had never slept with a man on the first date, and what she and this man had experienced together certainly didn't qualify as a date. So why had it felt so intimate? How could she be so affected—body, mind, perhaps soul, if she admitted that she believed in something so non-rational—by a casual encounter with a stranger she knew nothing about? She didn't know his name, hadn't seen his face. And that made it unlikely—impossible—that she would ever see him again . . . or recognize him if she did.

She wondered suddenly if, for all her caution, she had just made a terrible mistake. She'd managed to lose something she had never even had.

Chapter Four

Jacob Hunter threw down his book and sat up. His muscles were tense. As he swung his legs over the side of the king-sized bed, he felt a stab of pain. The muscles in his calves were so tight they seemed to vibrate like guitar strings. He walked stiffly to the bathroom and winced as he stepped into the shower.

The pain didn't surprise him. For the past weeks, he'd been pushing his body to the limit. But this feeling was different. He couldn't attribute it all to lactic acid in his quads. He felt keyed up. Preoccupied. The hot water sluicing over his shoulders couldn't relieve the knot in his chest. Even the muscles in his jaw felt like they were about to snap. He groaned and turned his face to the water. *Relax,* he told himself.

The criterium didn't start until five p.m., but Jacob had to be there hours early to warm up and check the course. The race would be short, intense, and dangerous. Sixty minutes of hard, technical riding through the streets of Vail. Though he hated to admit it, Jacob still felt a rush of nervous energy before every race. But even a case of the pre-race jitters couldn't explain this degree of agitation.

Jacob had more to worry about than his performance in the criterium. Usually, he raced like he had something to prove. This time, he'd be racing like he had something to hide. His number one priority was dodging the journalists that swarmed Vail like a plague of locusts. The irony of the situation wasn't lost on him. Once he actually craved the attention that the media lavished on football heroes and baseball stars. He'd wanted the fanfare, the acceptance. Cycling had never been popular in America. The sport had never received the appreciation it deserved. In Europe, Jacob was loved and hated. Loved for his raw talent, that mixture of grace and brutal strength that powered him through to a victory at the Paris-Roubaix. And hated for exactly the same thing.

He still remembered the sneering French television announcer who'd cried out in disdain and disbelief: "It cannot be! The *cowboy* has crossed the finish line! And the real cyclists are far behind!" The Europeans appreciated cycling but they had little appreciation for American cyclists winning their most treasured races. The Paris-Roubaix Classic was one of the continent's oldest and most important races. A good finish in the Paris-Roubaix separated the cyclists from the cycle-tourists. And winning . . .

Winning didn't mean you were good. Winning meant you were God.

Jacob remembered every second of the race. He'd thought his teeth were going to break as he rode across the cobblestones. His elbows turned to jelly. Sixty miles of pure pain. As well as the equally grueling, but less jolting sixty miles of pavement. When he'd gone down in the mud and scrambled up again with a gaping gash in his thigh, everyone was sure he was out of it. But in that final sprint, he'd outpaced not only the world champion cyclist, but his own body. His own dreams. He was moving beyond the speed of thought. Every fiber of his body was tearing. Burning up. He'd never been so close to dying. He'd never felt so alive.

It was the best day of his life. And nobody back home gave a damn.

However, in the past few months, things had changed. Some bigwig in L.A. had gotten the idea that cycling could be the next big thing—if the races had the right down home flavor and a spectacular, all-American venue. If there were an American face to put on the posters.

Jacob rubbed his hands over his face, tried to release the tension in his jaw. It was useless. He shut the tap, dried, and dressed. He glanced at the pile of newspapers on the table—his image graced the front page of every one.

It was almost funny. A year ago, he was on cloud nine. Winning the Paris-Roubaix. Catapulting to international fame. Best of all, becoming the poster boy at the center of an American cycling renaissance. He'd always wanted his country to embrace cycling. To recognize the sport for what it was. The ultimate test of the body and mind. The most beautiful sacrifice a man could ever make to speed. To freedom.

Now, he'd give anything to rewind the clock. To go back to the days when the French booed him in the streets. And the Americans . . . Well, the Americans didn't care enough to ignore him. They didn't even know he existed.

Thanks to the funds and enthusiasm of that L.A. bigwig, a new race had been born. A race modeled on the European classics but with an American twist. It would be bigger. Harder. Longer. It would take place in Colorado, starting only a few dozen miles from the town where Jacob grew up. And it was supposed to be a media firestorm.

Even today's criterium was just an excuse to drum up attention for the big race, now only ten days away. They were calling it the Colorado Classic. They were calling Jacob Hunter the hometown hero. And all eyes were on him, following his every move. He was jumping out of his skin with the pressure. Every second it got worse.

And yesterday, his sponsors had dropped a bomb.

They'd given a reporter permission to shadow him all through the next week leading up the Colorado Classic. They even wanted him to give an interview today. Before the criterium. They'd scheduled the meeting for noon in the hotel restaurant. As if Jacob could eat while he fielded the questions of a news hound determined to invade his carefully guarded privacy . . . what little there was left of it. He'd argued with the sponsors until he was hoarse, but they were determined to grab whatever share of the spotlight Jacob was offered by the American media. They sponsored athletes, they reminded him, for business reasons, not personal ones. Besides, they assured him, it would be nothing but a celebrity profile, a fluff piece. Little did they know how dangerous any attention could be for Jacob right now, even from the most star-struck of journalists.

His anger ebbed as the memory of his other preoccupation arose in his mind, bringing with it a flood of sensation throughout his whole body. The smell of a woman's hair, floral and fresh . . . the taste of her honey-sweet mouth . . . the feel of her firm, silky flesh under his hands . . . those outrageous curves he'd traced like a blind man. He couldn't stop himself. He tried to piece together the body he'd never seen in daylight. He was momentarily overwhelmed by the sensual recollection of that moment under the stars, when he and a stranger had fallen together into the feverish heat of one another's arms.

He so rarely had a moment to himself. He should have resented the fact that another hotel guest had invaded one of his only retreats. Instead he'd been tantalized by the unknown woman's presence, immediately drawn to her throaty voice, her lithe form slippery with water.

It had been sexually exciting, yes, but it had also stirred deeper feelings . . . feelings of exhilaration, of yearning. He remembered those feelings. He'd felt them during his first years of serious cycling as an adolescent, when he'd ventured further and further from his hometown of Leadville, Colorado, seeking out isolated stretches of highway, riding through mountain passes and alpine fields strewn with wildflowers. He got faster and faster, until he truly felt he was flying, alone and free. The pure love of speed kept him going, always looking for the long, sweeping descent on the far side of a pass or an unbroken straightaway on which he could pump his legs like pistons to bring himself closer and closer to pure velocity. The brutal grinds up the endless faces of Colorado peaks were worth it for those moments, however brief. Eventually he'd realized the climbs themselves were equally exhilarating in their own way. In the same way that any immense effort, however punishing, is satisfying when it achieves its goal.

Jacob left his room. He entered the elevator and punched the button for the lobby. He lifted himself up and down onto the balls of his feet, trying to expel his restless energy. He reminded himself of how far he'd come. He had achieved most of the goals he'd set for himself. At twenty-seven, he was in the best condition of his life, and he had the wins to prove it. Now he was back where he'd started . . . and it was a matter of pride that he dominate the field in the criterium and the upcoming Colorado Classic.

It should feel good to return home. To compete on his own landscape, the topography that had shaped his body, that had given him the drive to conquer the peaks of the Alps and the Pyrenees. It should feel good.

It didn't. He was in agony.

He sighed, feeling the weight of his stress descend again onto his shoulders. As he exited the elevator, he glanced at the clock on the wall and realized he was already late for his interview. His abdomen clenched. He felt less than certain that he could traverse the rocky terrain of a conversation with a reporter who wanted to write a profile about his life. Who wanted to expose him, all his private thoughts and concerns. Who wanted to make his secrets into her next headline.

Hell no.

In a split second, Jacob made his decision. He passed the entrance to the restaurant quickly but with his head up, as if daring anyone to stop him. Let the reporter sit there and wait. Suddenly, Jacob spotted the Directeur Sportif's assistant, Ben, coming into the lobby through the main doors.

"Hi Jake." Ben smiled. The lobby was dim, but Ben didn't remove his wraparound sunglasses. He broadened his cocky smile and pretended to shoot Jacob with his finger. Jacob forced a smile.

Normally, he'd rather take a real bullet than buddy around with Ben, but today was different. Today Ben might be of service.

"Playing chauffeur?" asked Jacob innocently. Ben often ferried equipment back and forth to races. He also ferried whoever the sponsors designated their current VIP. Usually some sporting goods tycoon they wanted to impress. Or a smarmy reporter.

Ben shrugged. "I'm the only guy around here that can handle four wheels."

"It's a burden, I know," said Jacob. "Listen, are you driving . . ." What was the reporter's name, again?

"Ariel Hayes," Ben supplied.

"Ariel Hayes," repeated Jacob. "To the race today?"

Ben folded his arms across his chest and looked at Jacob suspiciously. "Yeah," he said.

"Well, I'm going to give her a ride instead," said Jacob. "That way we can talk more. You can turn in your keys and spend the afternoon in the Biergarten."

In addition to being challenging races, criteriums doubled as citywide parties, with spectators mobbing the closed-off streets, drinking and shouting. Biergartens sprang up overnight. At the Mt. Hood criterium, the downtown had smelled like someone had opened a liquor-filled fire hydrant.

Strangely, Ben didn't look pleased to be discharged of his duty. Finally, he pulled off his sunglasses and gave Jacob a look that Jacob couldn't interpret. "Sure," he said. "See you at the race." As he turned away, Jacob could have sworn he winked.

What was that about? Were he and Ben involved in a pissing contest he wasn't aware of? It seemed like every interaction he had these days was tainted.

Except for last night.

No. He couldn't dwell on last night. It was as distant as a dream. Just made him feel worse.

At least he'd taken care of that reporter. He hoped Ariel Hayes waited for a good long time before she realized that Jacob Hunter wasn't going to show. How long before she realized her ride was similarly MIA?

Swinging easily through the front door, he examined his conscience for feelings of guilt. Nope. Reporters were vultures. As a cyclist, Jacob had to overcome challenges every day. Let Ariel Hayes fight for her interview. If she wanted to ask him questions so badly, she could chase him down. Maybe she would get a firsthand taste of the most important, the most *newsworthy*, thing about him.

He was very, very fast.

*

The Colorado air was cool and dry. Endlessly fresh. Breathing hard, Jacob sprinted through the final lap of the criterium. He'd dominated the race and was easily forty meters ahead of his closest competitor. He sat up on his bike and saluted before he'd even crossed the finish line. In response, the crowd went wild. Jacob heard screams and popping bottles and a chorus of female voices chanting his name. He bowed his head briefly over his handlebars, taking deep breaths.

Did it, he thought. Exhilaration mingled with relief. Someone was thrusting a magnum of champagne into his arms. Steven Fratello, one of his teammates, had already opened another magnum and was aiming the spuming bottle at Jacob's chest. Jacob felt the cool liquid hit his throat, spraying across his face and dripping down to soak his jersey. He licked his lips. The champagne tasted surprisingly sweet.

Steven seemed to read his mind. "Not as dry and light as the champagne at Roubaix?" he joked. "You turned into some kind of froggy snob? Used to the finer stuff?"

Jacob met Steven's fist with his own in a victory pound and

Steven took the opportunity to grip his hand and raise it high in the air. Mugging for the cameras. Jacob couldn't help but grin as the crowd responded. "You're still a ham, Fratello," he said.

"Give 'em what they want, Jacob baby," Steven shouted, shooting champagne into the crowd. "This is an *exhibition*. Exhibit something. Break out the six-pack."

Jacob had to laugh. Steven's light-hearted positivity always made him feel better. It was a relief to know he had a true blue friend in the competitive world of pro cycling. "Twelve-pack," he quipped back and tugged down the zipper of his jersey.

"That's better." Steven laughed. "You just decimated the criterium! You gotta look like a hero."

"I don't look like a hero?" asked Jacob.

"A minute ago you looked like you were involved in a hit-and-run with someone's grandma. But now you look okay."

"Okay?" Jacob had to wipe another burst of champagne from his eyes. "You trying to drown me?"

"I am trying to *deify* you, my friend," shouted Steven, head tipped up toward the dimming sky. He hooted and flung the magnum, tackling Jacob and dragging him off his bike.

"We're the best," Steven panted. "Enjoy it."

Jacob's body was still surging with adrenaline. Steven was right. He needed to stop worrying. Too bad it felt like the problems he'd managed to leave behind at the starting line were right there waiting at the finish.

Not now. Not now. Enjoy it, Hunter, he told himself. Jacob cracked his own magnum of champagne and soaked a howling Steven.

"All right, all right," Steven begged, warding him off. "Podium's getting cold."

Feeling happier than he had in a long time, Jacob went to receive his trophy. But up on the podium, his momentary elation faded quickly. The flashing bulbs, the fat-cat grins of his sponsor's representatives, the squealing women—he wanted out of there. Pushing through the throngs that swarmed the podium, he looked for the signs and banners that bore his name and the company he raced for. There were his people, such as they were. He barely felt the congratulatory thumps as he entered the little cordoned off area. He thrust his trophy and check at Ben.

"Put these in the RV," he muttered. He ducked behind the banners to change rapidly into his street clothes. His skin was still sticky with champagne—all he wanted was a shower and a rubdown. He had to get back to his hotel. Unfortunately, Vail was still in chaos from the race. Punch-happy brawlers were blocking the traffic patterns that the beleaguered police were trying desperately to reestablish. He pushed through the crowd, hoping his nondescript black t-shirt and jeans would provide enough of a disguise. He'd hardly gone five yards before a microphone thrust itself under his nose. A woman with frosted hair that looked harder and more protective than his helmet was staring at him through designer glasses. Her make-up was about three-inches deep.

"Another magnificent performance from Jacob Hunter," she exclaimed, blinking her thickly lashed eyes. "Jacob, you're causing quite the sensation in Vail."

"Great," he said, trying to move around her. Her cameraman was beaming a light into his face. He took a step and was almost clotheslined by the microphone wire. He stumbled and cursed. *That would look good. Breaking his collarbone evading the press.*

The reporter didn't seem to notice that he'd nearly sprawled onto the pavement. She closed the distance between them, still prattling. "Jacob, what would you say to people who wonder whether it's physically possible to achieve the kinds of times you've been clocking?"

He grunted, trying to shield his eyes from the light.

"Jacob, what would you say to people who think you're getting help?" She stepped even closer.

"Jacob Hunter," she said in ringing tones, "are you using EPO?"

EPO.

Those three letters hit Jacob like the prongs of an electrified trident. He still wasn't used to reporters in the U.S. knowing anything about cycling, let alone being versed in the technical terms associated with cycling's leading scandals. Hearing this woman rattle off the name of the sport's most notoriously abused performance enhancing drug was amazing. More amazing by far than the accusation. He'd become accustomed to that back in France.

Suddenly it occurred to him that this woman might very well be Ariel Hayes. She certainly wouldn't have any reason to like him, not after the stunt he'd pulled earlier in the day. Maybe he'd managed to turn his celebrity profiler into a witch hunter. His sponsors were gonna love this. He switched on the charm.

"I don't have anything to say to those people," he responded with a crooked grin. Experience had taught him that this grin was a lady-pleaser. "I'm not here to talk. I'm here to ride. I'm here to ride because I love it. I'm going to let my riding speak for me. I'll see you at the Classic. Excuse me." He pivoted and strode quickly in the other direction, ducking behind a row of press vans, and turning down the street where he'd parked his motorcycle.

There it was. Shining blackly in the gathering dusk. A Ducati Monster. He'd be able to maneuver through the downtown mayhem and slip back to his hotel. A hot shower and a visit to Bernadette, his soigneur. He couldn't wait.

He straddled his bike, settled his helmet into place, and started to roll it out into the street. At that very moment, a cherry red convertible squealed up beside him. The driver's side door flew open.

"Where's the criterium?" the woman shouted. Her voice was husky, urgent, and she nearly ran around the front of her car. She stood only a few feet away from him, her full breasts moving up and down against the thin fabric of her shirt. He put his feet down and steadied his bike, drinking her in.

She was striking. A cascade of unruly red locks fell to her shoulders. Longer strands brushed the tops of her breasts. Her hair made a startling frame for her high cheek-boned face, the milky white skin dusted with pale freckles. Her enormous green eyes were almond-shaped, fringed with thick lashes. Her lips were full, the bottom lip maddeningly so. He couldn't look at it without wanting to bite it. To take it between his teeth.

"The criterium," she was saying. "The criterium."

He'd forgotten she'd even asked him a question. Now those green eyes were turning to glimmering slits.

"Dammit," she growled, and turned away to get back into the car. He couldn't help but follow the slender length of her graceful legs up to where her lush, perfectly shaped bottom filled out the back of her tight, knee-length black skirt. His groin tightened. He raked a hand through his hair ruefully. He was reacting to her like a middle-schooler. Must be the adrenaline.

"Criterium's over," he called to her.

She wheeled around and stared at him across the hood of the car. Then she cursed again in that low, husky voice. Jacob kick-started the bike and it roared to life.

The woman had thrown open the door of her car, obviously furious. Suddenly, she shouted to him again, half in the door. "Who won?" she shouted.

He grinned, not the crooked grin. A genuine smile, the first real smile he'd managed in weeks. "I did," he answered. After doing everything in his power not to draw attention to himself, he couldn't believe what he was saying. But the look on her face was worth it. He closed his visor and opened the throttle.

Chapter Five

Ariel squealed to a halt in front of the gigantic glass and brass front doors of the Alpenhof. She was fuming with rage. First, she'd been stood up. Then she'd found herself without a ride to the race. She was pretty sure she knew who she could blame for that oversight. She'd rented a car and fought her way through traffic and pedestrian throngs only to find that she'd missed the race entirely.

To top it all off, when she'd finally encountered Jacob Hunter, it was completely by accident. He'd caught her totally off-guard. She'd looked frazzled and foolish, and he'd looked handsome as the devil himself, delivering an irresistibly impish grin before abandoning her on the street. Who did he think he was? Oh, right—the hottest star in international cycling. Ariel, however, refused to be intimidated. She would get her story—and do her damnedest to deflate Jacob Hunter's massively engorged ego while she was at it.

She threw her keys at the valet, too angry to feel guilty about the shocked look on his young, friendly face. Stalking into the lobby, she immediately identified Hunter's broad back on the far side of the lobby. He was leaning unconcernedly against a pillar, talking to a gorgeous, leggy blond woman in very short shorts and tough-looking hiking boots. Hunter's posture was casual, but the woman looked tense and angry. Ariel wondered if Jacob had stood her up, too. The blond woman turned her back on him and walked away. Hunter stood and looked around him before heading toward the elevators, in the opposite direction.

"Jacob Hunter?" Ariel called, stepping quickly after him, determined to overtake him before he could evade her again.

He turned toward her. "Was that you I heard laying down some rubber outside? You've got NASCAR potential." He grinned, resuming his position leaning against the pillar. Ariel slowed, her anger slipping away, leaving her feeling awkward, uncertain. He was so confident, so feline in his graceful, careless stance. The darkened strands of his blond hair fell over his forehead boyishly, skimming the tops of his cheekbones. His face was flushed from the race, and there was still a vivid excitement animating his chiseled features. His rippling muscles, his skin tanned golden from long days of outdoor training, all created the seamless impression of a man in top physical form, whose conditioning lent him not only power and athletic prowess, but grace and a kind of hyper-masculine beauty.

Ariel was unnerved. His smile seemed friendly, but he'd already proven that he had no respect for her in a professional capacity. Nevertheless, she couldn't help but respond to the bantering tone in his voice, the frank appraisal in his golden eyes. His presence was invigorating, exciting. Maybe she could make this work . . .

"Do you like female racers?" she asked him in the same light, flirtatious tone. She smiled at him, unable to resist the infectious charm of his boyish grin.

"Only if they're fast," he told her, smiling more broadly. Ariel felt an electric current crackling between their two bodies. Why was she so powerfully affected by his presence, given all she knew, and all she guessed, about the less savory aspects of his character?

"Name the top three female cyclists," Ariel challenged him, trying to feel out his attitude toward other professional women trying to operate in male-dominated fields. Hunter's smile faltered; he furrowed his brow as if searching for names he only vaguely remembered. Ariel nearly stamped her foot in frustration; it seemed he was as much of a chauvinist as she'd feared.

But then Jacob's face cleared, and he smiled again as confidently as before. "Easy," he said. "Jeannie Longo, Connie Carpenter-Phinney, Kristin Armstrong."

Ariel realized he'd psyched her out with his false display of uncertainty. She was thrown off-guard. When would she be able to establish a clear understanding of Jacob Hunter the man—his motivations, his desires, his weaknesses? The success of her project depended on her success in navigating the shifting terrain of this maddeningly unpredictable man's psyche, his relationships, his drives. So far, she couldn't have predicted the next thing he'd say or do if her life, and not just her career, had depended on it.

"Are you a race car driver?" he asked, his eyes twinkling.

"No," said Ariel tartly, tiring of their contretemps. "I'm a reporter. Ariel Hayes, with *Cycling Today*. I'm doing a profile on you."

Jacob's face clouded immediately. Seeing his reaction, but not willing to let him off the hook now that she had him dangling, she pressed her advantage. "You owe me an interview."

"I have plans," he told her brusquely, making no excuses for his no-show that morning.

Ariel blushed, thrown off-guard. "I didn't mean now," she said.

"Right. So, have your people talk to my people—isn't that how it's done?" Jacob turned and walked away without another word. Ariel was flabbergasted. How had she managed to turn him against her so quickly? *This guy has a real problem with reporters,* she thought ruefully. She'd known Jacob Hunter was arrogant and unapproachable but she'd thought he couldn't be worse than a congressman with a secret taste for prostitutes or a religious leader who embezzled from his congregation. She was wrong. This was on another level.

Ariel prided herself on her intuitive understanding of other people's secret motivations—the greed, lust and love of power they tried to hide from the rest of the world. And she had a feeling Jacob was hiding something big. Something he'd do just about anything to hide.

Including walk away from the most sexually charged flirtation Ariel had experienced in years.

Except for last night in the pool.

Ariel tried to smother the memory even as it arose. That wasn't a flirtation. That was . . . *crazy.* Like something from a dream. Something that happened to other girls. A beautiful fluke, a moment of connection under the stars . . . She'd never thought she'd feel such an intense, sensual bond to another person, definitely not so quickly, definitely not with a person she didn't know, a person she hadn't even really *seen*. And now, here she was again, with her body responding uncontrollably to Jacob Hunter!

I should have stayed at sea level, she thought wryly. *I must be lightheaded up here.* She squared her shoulders. Well, be that as it may, she wasn't giving up. She wouldn't let her hormones and Jacob Hunter's bad attitude take her down so easily. No matter how nasty Jacob got, Ariel could handle it. She'd find a way in.

Maybe sooner than later, she thought as she turned and saw Ben, the assistant to the DS who'd picked her up at the airport, swaggering into the lobby. He had a package under his arm. When he saw her, he veered from his original course and came toward her with a broad grin on his face.

"Hey, beautiful," he said. "Enjoy the race?"

Ariel winced. This guy clearly thought he was God's gift to women. But at least it was a weakness she could exploit. Plastering what she hoped was a seductive smile on her unwilling face, she said sweetly, "Loved it. What's that you've got there?"

"Fan mail for the Big Man." Ben rolled his eyes and Ariel tried to look sympathetic. Clearly, Ben had issues when it came to Jacob Hunter. Well, what guy wouldn't be jealous of that body?

That body. Michelangelo could have taken a cue from Jacob Hunter.

Even the thought of Jacob's lean, impossibly muscled physique took her breath away. Which was not good. Not good at all. Ariel hoped she wasn't blushing. "Do you know where Jacob is?" she asked Ben. "We were supposed to meet up, but I think we got our signals crossed about where."

Ben looked at her speculatively. It was obvious that a lot of women asked Ben about Jacob. But Ariel had nothing in common with those Italian models and ski bunnies. She was different. She had an assignment. This was business. Jacob's looks, however undeniably sexy, were absolutely one hundred percent irrelevant.

"The lady doth protest too much . . ."

Ariel's father used to quote the Hamlet line whenever Ariel's over-vehement denials set off his alarm bells. He'd say it drily, arms crossed. What he'd meant was, *Ariel, you're not fooling anyone.*

Ben grinned and said simply, "Sure, I know where he is. I can lead you right to him."

In the elevator, Ariel wondered what she had gotten herself into. Ben held his peace, but he was still smirking at her in a way she didn't like at all. As the floor numbers flashed by, she considered telling Ben she'd changed her mind. She'd catch up with Jacob tomorrow. After all, she doubted he'd be happy to see her again so soon after his hostile departure from their conversation. Maybe it would be better to let sleeping dogs lie. At least for the night. She could regroup. Come up with a new strategy. Or just order room service and take a bath.

Too late.

The elevator doors opened and Ariel followed Ben down the hall. "Where are we going?" she asked, but Ben didn't answer.

He rapped lightly on the door at the end of the hall. The door wasn't fully closed, and as Ben pushed it open, Ariel saw the answer to her question. It was Jacob's hotel suite. Even grander than Ariel's, positioned so that the enormous windows of the central room looked out over the mountains. Ben called out, "Got your mail!" and a voice from the bedroom replied, "Bring it in here." Gesturing with his head for her to follow him, Ben led Ariel into the next room.

Ariel couldn't believe her eyes. Jacob Hunter was lying on his back on a massage table. He was stark naked, except for a towel—a very small towel—positioned between his legs like a loincloth. A middle-aged woman with thick eyebrows and the physique of a wrestler was briskly massaging his legs. Ariel watched, mesmerized, as the jostling motion of the massage threatened to shake the towel entirely out of position. She was unable to tear her eyes away from the sight of Jacob's perfect, smooth, golden body, revealed for her in all its glory. His shoulders were broad, his waist and hips narrow. He was covered head to toe in lean, hard muscle. His abdomen was like an anatomy study. Ariel wanted to touch it.

Her open-mouthed stare and deep blush had not passed unnoticed. The thickset woman had stopped her massage to look inquiringly at her. Ben was watching her with a glint of malicious humor in his eyes, enjoying every second of her discomfiture. She'd been set up.

"Ummm . . . " she stuttered. Mercifully, her cell phone sounded from the depths of her bag and she fumbled for it. "So sorry," she said, a trifle breathlessly. "It's New York. Business. I have to take this." She backed through the bedroom door, denying the call even as she pretended to answer it.

"Fax?" she said brightly. "No, I didn't get that fax."

Just before she made her escape from the bedroom, Jacob turned his head and opened his eyes to look at her—golden eyes that pierced her like lasers. She gave him a little wave, then covered the mouthpiece of the phone. "We'll catch up tomorrow," she said, in what she hoped was a professional, no-nonsense voice. She tripped a little over the doorframe and turned quickly, fighting to keep from breaking into an undignified run. She could hear the sound of male laughter—Ben? Jacob?—drifting after her.

Back in her room, she tried to calm herself down with breathing exercises and, when that didn't work, a stiff drink from the mini fridge. How could she have embarrassed herself so completely?

She wondered if she'd ever be able to face Jacob Hunter again. Yes, she told herself sternly. She would be. Because she had to be. Because it was her job. She would continue her investigations tomorrow, as she'd planned. And she would pretend that nothing had happened. Mustering her resolve (and slugging the rest of her drink) she sat down to write up her notes for the day.

*

After his massage, Jacob met Liz, as they'd planned, for a quiet dinner at a modest—but amazingly delicious—Italian restaurant he'd discovered a few years ago. He hadn't been sure Liz would show; she'd been furious with him earlier at the hotel. She was a ski instructor who lived in Vail year-round, hiking and mountain biking during the summer. They'd had an on-again, off-again relationship whenever he was in town. It was casual, low-pressure. Exactly what Jacob was looking for.

Lately, however, Liz had seemed to want more. She'd hinted that she'd be willing to travel to spend more time him. And she was often angry about something. Like today, when she'd dressed him down for an imagined offense.

In the soft candlelight, she was beautiful, with strong, aristocratic features, blond hair to her waist, legs a mile long. She'd changed out of her sporty daytime attire into a simple black dress and strappy heels. With a twinge of regret, Jacob realized he couldn't string her along, couldn't allow her to believe he could be anything to her but a friend-with-benefits. Liz was talking about mountain biking, a subject that used to hold his interest.

" . . . sweet single-track . . . " she was saying, gesturing with her fork as she talked animatedly.

He nodded, dipping his bread in a dish of high-quality green-hued olive oil. Then he noticed that she was looking at him expectantly. "What?" he asked, and she dealt him a scathing glare.

"Do you want to ride this trail with me?" she repeated in a harsh tone. Then she brushed her hair out of her face and smiled a tight, brittle smile. "I mean, it's beautiful. It has some climbs that I think you'd love. And then we can relax in the hot tub with some vino. We haven't done that in ages."

"Ummmm." He dipped another piece of bread in the oil, searching his brain for a plausible excuse. He used to love casual rides with Liz through the mountains. But suddenly it seemed heavy. It seemed like she was judging his every word, every action, for a sign of commitment. "We'll have to play it by ear," he said. "I'm on a strict training schedule for the Classic."

"Training involves taking it easy the week before a race," she said acidly. "Unless I've missed some new discovery in sports medicine."

"And I've got these sponsor chores," Jacob continued, evading her eyes. "Interviews. Promo stuff."

"Covering your body in oil and standing at the mall?" Liz rolled her eyes. She pushed away her plate of risotto. "Fine. Just let me know, okay? I'll keep my schedule free until I hear from you."

"Great," said Jacob woodenly. He told himself that it was the pressure that was triggering his negative response. But it wasn't just Liz's demands on his time. As he looked at her across the table, another face superimposed itself on hers . . . one with more delicate features, higher coloring, surrounded by flame colored curls . . .

Jacob remembered the enticing way the rosiness had spread across Ariel's cheeks and throat as she'd stared down at him in his bedroom. He'd given many interviews while getting massaged— in fact, it was during post-race sessions with their soigneurs that cyclists were most likely to be interviewed. But from the look on Ariel's face, you'd have thought she didn't know this scenario was a common occurrence in her line of work. Maybe she was new to *Cycling Today.* Or maybe she was responding to him as more than just a journalist. Maybe she was responding to him as a woman. The thought made him grin. Liz saw his features light up and reached for his hand across the table. He returned her gentle squeeze half-heartedly.

"There's my Jacob," she said. "Now that I've got you back with me, I don't want anything to come between us."

After dinner, Liz asked him to come home with her. Jacob made excuses. A long day, exhaustion from the race. "I'm really bushed," he said, the cliché tripping on his tongue. He almost winced at the false ring.

Liz looked at him incredulously. Then her face turned stormy. "I've noticed that you're looking a little out of shape," Liz said, that harsh quality creeping back into her voice. Her expression mingled anger and disappointment. "I'm sure the criterium was very difficult for you," she added. "I heard Steven had to pull you most of the way."

Jacob understood that she was lashing out because she was hurt. But it didn't make her mean streak any easier to take. He cursed his own clumsiness. He had to admit he probably wasn't handling the situation very well at all. He kissed her cheek as he said goodbye.

"I'll call you," he said and she muttered something unintelligible. He figured he was better off not trying to figure it out.

Back at the hotel, he was restless—tired but unable to relax. He had three women vying for space in his thoughts—Liz, Ariel . . . and the mysterious woman he'd found in the hotel pool. As if he didn't have enough on his mind already. He scrolled through the dialed numbers on his cell phone, suddenly ready to make the call he'd been putting off since his fight with Brian at the Penalty Box.

It was far too late, of course. He listened to the phone ring on and on and on. He'd have to call back during the daytime. He dropped the phone onto the bedspread, rubbed a hand over his face. The muscles in his neck felt as though they were tightening.

Was he ever going to be able to relax?

He found himself, without having consciously chosen to do so, collecting a towel and exiting into the hotel corridor, entering the elevator, punching the button for the rooftop . . .

When he stepped from the elevator onto the marble tiled rooftop, the stars were as brilliant as they'd been last night. The moon was fuller, hanging like a pearl above the twinkling lights of the town in the valley. But there was no one else there. Realizing how much he'd wanted to find someone floating in the pool— someone who was still a stranger, but somehow intimately known to him—Jacob was filled with disappointment. Approaching the pool's edge, his eye was caught by a glint of metal on the tile. Stooping, he picked up a tiny object and examined it as well as he could in the moonlight.

As far as he could make out, it was a piece of gold jewelry—a little charm in the shape of a book. Something a woman would wear as a pendant or on a bracelet. Could it be a clue to the identity of the woman he'd nearly made love to in exactly this spot one night earlier?

Jacob slipped the charm into his pocket.

Chapter Six

Jacob finished stretching and sat for a moment on the grass at the bottom of the enormous hill in the shady northeast corner of the park. The park was on the outskirts of town and not nearly as well tended or attractive as some of the other parks he knew of in the area, but his coach hadn't picked this park for its scenic appeal. He'd picked it for the killer climb. Jacob's practiced eye could appreciate the slope before him in all its brutal majesty. A path led through the tall grass and the towering pines, a straight shot up the hill, which blended seamlessly into the higher mountains that loomed above Vail. It was the kind of long, steep hill that joggers walked up, and that casual cyclists gave up on within a few yards. Jacob had ten sprints to go. Then he'd be finished with his last day of hard training.

Liz had been right, of course. For the week leading up to the Classic, he'd be taking it easy. Of course, "easy" was relative. For Jacob, it certainly didn't mean parking himself with potato chips in front of the television. He'd be riding nearly every day, but for only a few hours. He wouldn't be driving his body to the limit. Instead, he'd be storing up power, allowing the muscles he'd worked ruthlessly in the past weeks to repair themselves in preparation for the supreme effort he'd be putting forth during the Classic. He loved the hard training, as painful as it could be, but he was looking forward to spending a few days riding at an easy pace through the beautiful Colorado landscape. He wanted to enjoy the solitary hours. He wanted a chance to think. To dream. He was rarely alone these days.

Sorry, Liz, he said to himself, remembering her desire to mountain bike with him. He wouldn't be taking her up on her offer. He wanted time to himself. He stood, put on his helmet, swung a leg over his bicycle. He took a breath and readied himself to climb the hill at top speed.

*

"Hey there," called Ben. He was walking out of Covered Bridge Coffee in Vail Village. Ariel noted his signature smirk and had to fight to keep from rolling her eyes.

"Hey there," she called back, tossing her purchases through the window of the rental car. She'd bought snacks to keep her blood sugar up while she tracked down Brian Jenks, as well as a road map of Colorado. So far, she hadn't been able to find out much about the man who'd brawled so publicly with Jacob Hunter, but she hadn't done much digging, just asked a few local teens in criterium t-shirts if they'd read about the fight. Blank stares for that effort. Oh well. Random cold questioning wasn't exactly a topnotch journalistic technique. She figured a trip to the scene of the fight in Minturn would yield some juicy information.

By all accounts, Minturn was a depressed place, a mining town not far from the ritzier Vail. Ariel knew from experience that the friends you leave behind in hometown haunts can resent the hell out of you if you have the guts or the luck to get out. Now that Jacob Hunter was an international star, maybe his presence wasn't exactly appreciated back in his old stomping grounds. Maybe the working guys in towns like Minturn, Redcliff, and Leadville were itching to teach Jacob a lesson about where he belonged.

But why would a man in Jacob Hunter's position hang out in a hardscrabble bar so trouble could bite him in the ass? It didn't make sense. Unless he'd been so hopped up on drugs he'd needed a chance to act out his aggressive energy. Ariel had heard of athletes on steroids doing terrible things—hurting their wives, their children. Performance enhancing drugs were no joke. Maybe Hunter had needed an outlet and Brian Jenks was in the wrong place at the wrong time. Or maybe Brian Jenks and Jacob Hunter had a history. If so, Ariel planned on getting the history from Jenks. She had a hunch that Jenks's version would be more to her readers' taste. After all, *X-Ray* was a magazine that prided itself on exposing the corrupt inner workings of corporations, the government, and now, professional sports.

Jacob Hunter was hiding something. She needed to find out the details. ASAP. The sooner she could turn in her article the better. Any contact she had with Jacob Hunter made things too . . . complicated.

"Can I get you a cup of coffee?" Ben was asking. Ariel frowned. She didn't feel like wasting time with Ben. She wanted to get to Minturn. She looked at Ben again and hesitated. She could ask him where Jacob was training today and put off going to Minturn until later in the week. But she wasn't sure if she'd trust Ben to give a straight answer.

No, she decided, better to go to Minturn. She'd try to catch Jacob later, at the hotel. She'd call his room and have him meet her for a cocktail and an interview. *After* he'd finished with his soigneur and put his clothes back on. Before Ariel could formulate a polite rejection, Ben started waving his free arm over his head.

"Fratello, Henderson," he shouted, and two muscular young men crossed over to Ben and Ariel's side of the street. Ariel didn't need to be told that these guys were cyclists. She was starting to recognize the type.

Muscular. Gorgeous. And with that unmistakably arrogant swagger.

The one Ben called Fratello was dark haired with lively brown eyes. Henderson was blond with California good looks. They high-fived Ben then introduced themselves to Ariel. Steven Fratello. Randall Henderson. Teammates of Jacob Hunter.

"Ariel Hayes," said Ariel.

"Aren't you the reporter profiling Jake?" asked Randall.

"How's that going?" laughed Steven, brown eyes dancing.

Ariel laughed back. "Not well," she admitted. "He stood me up for our interview."

"Jake's a prickly bastard," said Steven. "I think it's a little weird for him to be back in Colorado. He's from here, you know."

"I know," said Ariel. "I did do *some* research on my subject."

"Sorry," said Steven. "I forget that anyone in the States knows anything about cycling."

"In Paris, we're famous," said Randall with a cocky smile. "I got finger-cramps from all the autographing."

"Well, you have a very long name," said Ariel with a straight face.

Steven shot her an appraising glance. A grin tugged at the corner of his mouth. Ariel found that she liked him. He definitely had a sense of humor.

"Look," said Steven. "Jake's not good with reporters. He's a private guy. Don't take it personally."

"I don't want to pry into his life," said Ariel, with a twinge of guilt. "I just want to introduce his fans to the man behind . . . "

"The spandex?" broke in Steven, that mischievous twinkle in his eyes disarming Ariel completely.

"Thanks, but I've already had the pleasure," said Ariel and heard Ben snort. From the grins that Steven and Randall exchanged, Ariel was willing to bet they'd heard plenty about her undignified exit from Jacob's hotel suite.

"Right now, Jake's *killing* the hill in Packer Park," said Steven. "You should check it out. I think you'll understand more about Jake if you see him ride. Also, he can't give you too much of a hard time if he's out of breath."

Why was Steven being so helpful? Ariel felt a surge of gratitude, followed by another, more pronounced twinge of guilt. If this friendly teammate knew what she was really up to, he wouldn't be so open.

"Jake's a great cyclist," said Steven seriously, looking Ariel straight in the eyes. "It's exciting to see him ride. Go to the park. Check him out. Good publicity for Jake is good publicity for cycling. He's the best the sport has to offer. You can quote me on that."

Ariel saw the unmistakable sincerity in the man's face. "I will," she said. "Thanks." With this opportunity handed to her, she realized that Minturn could wait.

Glancing at that map as she drove her sporty rental car to the park, she thought about what Steven Fratello had said. He clearly respected Jacob Hunter. He wasn't just giving her the party line. Did he really think that Jacob was winning his races without drugs? Or were drugs such a ubiquitous part of cycling that he didn't discount Jacob's triumphs even though he was using? Ariel had a thing or two to learn about how the tight-knit cycling community operated.

She parked her car and set out to locate the path that Jacob would be riding up and down. When she found it, she began to walk uphill alongside it—and was amazed by its length and the steepness of its slope.

This might be a park, but Jacob is hardly on a picnic, she thought. Even after walking for several minutes at a brisk pace—enjoying the slight increase in her heart rate and the deep breaths of clean mountain air scented with pine needles she had to take to maintain it—Jacob was nowhere in sight.

Then she saw him. And nearly as soon as she saw him, he was alongside her—then past her. He rocketed by like a cannonball, coming downhill faster than she would have thought possible. So fast she felt the wind of his passing. As blazingly quickly as he was going, he looked poised, balanced. In perfect control.

She couldn't keep herself from imagining those muscular arms around her. What would it feel like to be handled by someone whose body was so exquisitely tuned? Sensitive but powerful.

Right. That's the story my readers want. Ariel groaned, disgusted with herself, trying to stifle her thoughts. *I'll just write an ode to Jacob Hunter's overwhelming hotness.* She kept walking uphill, knowing he'd be coming past her again eventually. Her thigh muscles started to burn. She was due for some exercise herself.

Within a few minutes—much more quickly than she'd expected—she looked back to see Jacob toiling up the hill. She was amazed by the speed he was able to maintain in spite of the punishing grade. His skintight spandex outlined every curve and plane of his amazing body. His thighs and calves bulged with power as he drove the pedals in their constrained circuit, defying gravity with every stroke. The muscles of his torso showed in clear outline through the fabric of his jersey. His biceps and forearms tensed as he gripped the handlebars, leaning forward and attacking the hill as if he held a grudge against it. He was sweating profusely, his skin shining in the sunlight. He was beautiful. And dangerously strong. His damp hair hung into his eyes, which were singularly focused, intense. Completely unaware of her presence. It was only when he came within a few feet of her that Jacob noticed her standing awestruck by the side of the path. Without slowing, Jacob grunted at her out of the side of his mouth, "Last rep. Meet you at the bottom." Then he was away, moving steadily up the hillside at a fast clip.

Ariel couldn't help but stare at him as he rode away from her, appreciating the view from behind as much as the one from the front. His narrow waist and tight backside swayed to the rhythm of his pedal stroke. His back swarmed with muscles, gliding against one another like sinuous snakes. And his legs . . . Ariel tore her eyes away, aware of a growing heat in her belly and a flush of warmth as blood rose in her face and her nipples tightened.

Journalistic objectivity, she reminded herself sternly, and started down the hill.

*

Jacob crested the top of the hill, then turned and shot back down. He sluiced himself with water from his squirt bottle, his jersey unzipped to the waist. He was breathing hard, his legs pulsing with blood, his helmet off and his BMC bicycle laid down on its side. He wasn't sure how he was going to deal with Ariel in this condition. He always felt great after his workouts, keyed up with endorphins. But the subsequent relaxation and fatigue could put him in a vulnerable state.

As she walked down the hill, Ariel's hair and body were backlit by the sun. Light shone through the nimbus of her hair and threw her voluptuous curves into silhouette. Jacob had rarely seen a woman with such a perfect body—perfect for his tastes, at least. He tended to associate with female athletes. Some were almost sexless, their bodies honed to the point of total androgyny. Some more casual athletes like Liz, maintained a feminine body type. But Jacob had rarely encountered Ariel's particular blend of lushness and strength, someone who was as womanly as she was toned. She had the most perfect posture he'd ever seen. She carried herself like a queen. Her motions were incredibly graceful. She had the kind of agility that Jacob knew required massive core strength. Her limbs were long and supple. But her hips, her bottom, round as a peach, her large, high breasts . . . Words failed.

The models he'd met in the course of his photo shoots, supposedly the most beautiful women in the world, some of whom seemed determined to make him into a bedmate, looked like badly drawn stick figures in comparison.

Jacob tightened his jaw. He couldn't afford to treat this woman as anything but a threat. Couldn't afford to respond to her the way his body was already responding . . .

*

As Ariel walked closer, she wondered what she could have done to Jacob to make him glare at her like that. Was he upset that she'd shown up at his training? Or that she'd disrupted his massage the day before? Stifling the stirrings of self-doubt that his forbidding look inspired, she squared her shoulders and planted herself in front of him, trying to ignore her visceral reaction to his presence, the heat he gave off like a furnace, the jersey open over his broad chest and tightly muscled stomach, the smell of his healthy, salty sweat . . . Unbidden, her eyes fell to his groin and she gasped. The spandex of his shorts hid nothing . . . *nothing.*

Jacob Hunter was fantastically well-endowed.

Rendered speechless, Ariel was relieved to see that Jacob looked equally distracted. He was staring intently at . . . her wrist? Her bracelet?

Her father had given her the gold charm bracelet for her sixteenth birthday, with three charms attached. A tiny book. A ballet shoe. A heart. For balance, he said, and for love. She knew he didn't mean the kind of balance she practiced at the barre. From then on he'd given her another charm for each passing birthday— five more while he was alive. He'd given her eight charms in all, and she'd bought a few more for herself, as a way of remembering him. She played with the bracelet when she was thinking, rubbing the charms between the thumb and middle finger of her opposite hand. The older charms had been smoothed by her touch over the years until their contours faded, the embossed details becoming less distinct, the metal more burnished, mellowed.

Ariel and Jacob's eyes met. To Ariel's surprise, they both flushed.

*

It was *her.* Jacob felt a wordless confusion. Ariel Hayes. The woman who'd been haunting him. The woman with whom he'd shared those moments of raw, naked honesty on the hotel rooftop. She'd felt his body's hunger, his need for connection, for intimacy. And he'd felt hers. The blood rushed to his groin as he remembered the feel of her slippery, silky skin, the way her curvaceous body had melted against him, the luscious wetness he'd felt when he slipped his fingers into her lace panties and touched the petal-soft folds of her sex. Holding her eyes—knowing his cycling shorts did nothing to hide his sudden arousal—he smiled in spite of himself.

*

Ariel was surprised by the sudden sweetness of that smile. And she had no idea what had caused it. To call this man "mercurial" would be an understatement. She could only hope that his good mood lasted for the time it would take her to establish a rapport— or at least to ask him a few key questions.

"Jacob," she said, and was surprised to hear the caressing tone in her own voice. She'd always made it a point of honor not to use the kind of feminine wiles that some female journalists deployed in their pursuit of a story. But, truth be told, she'd never felt this way about a subject. The hint of seduction in her voice and in her body language didn't feel like a strategy, wasn't something she'd planned. It came all too naturally.

"You know I'd like to interview you," she continued, "but the fact is, readers want to see you as a complete individual, not just a racer. I loved watching you train just now. But I need to see you off the bike, as well. So I can give your public a sense of the man behind the sport. They already know Jacob Hunter, the athlete. They're hungry for more."

Jacob's eyes flashed challengingly. "The real Jacob Hunter, huh?" He smiled. "Are you sure they can handle it?"

"I guess we'll find out." Ariel smiled back, unable to resist his playful good humor.

Jacob reached out and clasped Ariel's wrist with his calloused hand. Ariel gasped. The contact—skin to skin—was like an electric shock. He pulled her gently toward him. "Come with me," he said softly.

Ariel wondered what she'd gotten herself into. And she wondered if she cared. "My rental car's in the parking lot," she said, trying not to let him see how his casual touch had startled her. "Where do you want to go? I can follow you."

"Leave the car. We'll throw my bike in the back and pick it up later. Ride with me on the motorcycle. We'll go change at the hotel." His gaze raked her up and down; Ariel suddenly felt naked, exposed.

"I need to shower. You need to look less citified. I'm going to take you out and show you the local color. You need to put on something . . . more casual." He smiled. Ariel glanced down at her sleeveless white silk blouse, her narrow black pants, her Prada flats, bought on clearance. In New York, and most other cities on the Eastern seaboard, you had to look serious to be taken seriously. Serious meant designer. Ariel had combed the sale racks and the consignment stores to build her professional wardrobe on a shoestring. But apparently things worked differently in the West.

Jacob dropped her wrist to shoulder his bike. Ariel missed the tingling sensation he'd transmitted to her through her fingers. She followed him obediently to the parking lot, where he removed the front wheel of his bike and laid the frame across her back seat. She wondered if he worried that it would be stolen. She was sure it was fantastically expensive.

Apparently not. He walked away from it without a backward glance, leaving Ariel to lock the car.

"Um, Jacob," she asked, "how did you get both the bicycle and the motorcycle here at the same time?"

Jacob smiled. "I drove the motorcycle. Ben met me with the bike. It gets worked over most nights. We can get him to pick it up later, too. Leave your car keys at the front desk for him."

Ariel smiled a lopsided grin, one that felt more genuine than any of the other smiles she'd produced during the course of this assignment. The others had all been designed to produce a response. "So he's good for something, after all?" she asked archly.

Jacob glanced back, surprised by her obvious sarcasm, then barked a laugh when he saw the expression on her face. "Actually," he said, "he's basically worthless. An errand boy who likes to think of himself as a mover and shaker. Since no one on the up-and-up takes him seriously, he's drawn to the dark side. If you need something sketchy, underhanded, or illegal, he's your man. Assuming he doesn't mess it up."

Ariel's smile dropped as suddenly as it had come. Was there a significance to Jacob's words he hadn't intended? Could Ben be responsible for supplying Jacob with drugs? She remembered the package he'd carried to Jacob's suite the day before. Mail? Or contraband pharmaceuticals?

She tried to pull herself together and marshal the whirl of thoughts and questions in her mind into something like a plan. Then she stopped short. There was another factor here she hadn't considered.

Ariel had never ridden a motorcycle before.

"Don't I need a helmet?" she asked nervously.

"You can wear mine. I'll wear this one." Strapping his bike helmet under his chin, he climbed on the motorcycle and grinned at her, posing.

Ariel burst out laughing. He looked ridiculous in his cycling kit and bike helmet, straddling the big motorcycle and smiling up at her roguishly. Maybe Jacob Hunter didn't take himself so seriously after all.

"Come on," he said, his voice suddenly husky, and he caught her wrist again and pulled her body against him. Ariel had no choice but to swing her leg over the bike and settle herself tightly against Jacob's warm, hard back.

Electric. She caught her breath. The feeling was electric.

Her breasts were crushed against him. She wrapped her arms around his waist. He felt like he was made of something more than flesh—like smooth wood, or polished metal. He started the motorcycle and the vibration traveled through her, humming between their bodies. She sighed involuntarily.

"Ready?" Jacob asked. She realized her fingers were kneading his jersey anxiously.

"Ready," she said. They pulled out. Ariel half-expected some daredevil burst of speed. Instead, Jacob drove slowly. Cautiously. Mindful of her nervousness.

"Too fast?" Jacob turned his face to shout above the engine. Ariel gripped him even tighter. The unexpected consideration caused her heart to flutter. Suddenly, she felt invulnerable. She looked down at the pavement moving beneath them. She thought she felt a hint of what Jacob must feel cycling, pushing himself harder and harder against the wind. Or what she'd felt, dancing.

Like dreams she had as a little girl. Dreams of flying. She almost cried out at the sheer joy of it.

"Faster!" she cried and leaned with him effortlessly as they roared around the last curve of the park road. Together they sped through the streets of Vail.

Back at the hotel, Ariel still felt like she was in a dream. She changed into jeans and a green t-shirt. She glanced at herself critically in the mirror. "How's this for casual?" she said to herself. She pulled her unruly hair into a loose ponytail and went to meet Jacob in the lobby. When she saw him waiting for her in cowboy boots, worn out jeans, and a thin, soft-looking t-shirt, she stopped in her tracks. His hair was still wet from the shower and a slow smile spread across his face as she came toward him.

*

"You dress down nice," he said. It was true. In faded jeans and a simple tee, Ariel had a natural glow. She looked less prissy, less like an uptight New York reporter with a Blackberry addiction. She looked ready for a casual conversation over a cold beer. Which, frankly, he preferred to an inquest in a brightly lit hotel restaurant.

Yes, this would be better. The two of them, relaxed, hanging out in a laid back environment. He could tell her just enough to keep her satisfied, without betraying anything important. Casual conversation. That was the key. Except for one problem. He hated to admit it, but he already wanted more than casual conversation. He wanted her in his bed. He wanted to talk to her seriously without worrying about what she'd write down. He wanted to lie with her under the stars and feel, again, that moment of connection. A sexual excitement linked to something deeper.

He hadn't felt this way for a very, very long time. Maybe never.

But Ariel Hayes wasn't a mystery woman—a rooftop mermaid—appearing out of nowhere and vanishing just as quickly. She was a reporter. He had to remember that. Anything he said to her would be fair game. He had to be on guard. He had to remember not to say anything about what was really on his mind.

Damn, she was beautiful.

"Let's get out of here," he said gruffly. He wished he could forget about Jacob the cyclist and Ariel the reporter. He wanted to relate to her man to woman.

Well, at least he could pretend for a little while. Just for tonight. Luckily, he knew the right place.

*

After a thrilling ride outside the limits of Vail Village, Jacob turned into a large parking lot filled with pickup trucks and motorcycles. Ariel hopped off the bike.

"Sweet Rose-Marie," said Jacob and whistled. Ariel looked around. The blond from the other day? Was she Rose-Marie? But then she took in the low, sprawling building with a huge buzzing sign: a grizzly bear lit-up in neon and "Rose-Marie's" spelled out in blinking red letters. Jacob dealt Ariel another heart-stopping grin.

"She taught me to two-step," he explained.

"You two-step?"

Jacob pulled her to him and whirled her around in the parking lot. Ariel saw the lights spin overhead.

"That's not the two-step!" she protested breathlessly.

"So I don't two-step," admitted Jacob. "I square-danced though. In gym class. Third grade. Tabor Elementary."

"I'll be sure to mention your square-dancing days in my article," Ariel said.

"Square-dancing always made me dizzy." Jacob laughed, releasing her. "It wasn't really my thing."

"Dizzy, huh?" It was hard to imagine Jacob off-balance.

"How about you?" he asked, lifting her hand above her head and twirling her around. Ariel completed the turn, then stepped away from him and shrugged.

"I don't get dizzy," she said. She brushed a stray strand of hair from her face and felt the heat of his gaze as his eyes followed the curve of her arm back to where her soft green t-shirt clung to her full breasts.

She stepped forward into fourth position, then whipped her body around in a double pirouette.

"See?" she said, relishing the astonished look on his face.

"Walk a straight line after that," Jacob dared her, and Ariel began walking smartly to the bar's entrance.

Oh God, he's looking at my ass, she thought.

As they walked into Rose-Marie's he put his arm around her shoulder.

"Did you do ballet?" he asked.

"Only in gym class," she replied.

"Ha," he said. They sat at a booth. Couples two-stepped in an open space by the bar. Over in the back, past the pool tables, a crowd surrounded a mechanical bull, now in the process of tossing a heavy-set young man into the air. Ariel winced as he hit the ground.

"You're not much for straight answers, are you?" observed Jacob. Ariel stared at him across the table.

"I'm a reporter," she said. "I prefer to ask the questions."

"That's one thing we have in common, then," said Jacob, leaning forward. He brushed his fingers across her wrist. He lightly touched one of the charms on her bracelet. "This is beautiful," he said seriously. "I'd ask who gave it to you, but . . ."

"But I'm the one who's interviewing *you*," Ariel finished. Her pulse was leaping. His fingers still rested lightly on her wrist.

"We have more in common than you think," she said suddenly. She didn't know she was going to say the words until she heard them coming out her mouth.

"Oh yeah?" Jacob was looking at her even more intently. His brown eyes bored into hers. If he weren't so distractingly good looking she'd be able to think before she spoke. At least she wasn't stuttering.

"I starting studying ballet when I was three years old," Ariel said. "I went to New York City to dance at Julliard. The plan was to join a company. Travel the world."

"What happened?" asked Jacob. Ariel closed her eyes briefly. The memory still caused her pain.

"I broke a bone in my foot," she said. "I couldn't dance for months. When you're at the top of your field, working your body as hard as you can, a few months . . ."

"Can mean everything," said Jacob, with a strange light in his eyes.

"It's amazing how long it takes to get to where you want to be. How long it takes to make your body work the way you want it to work . . . and then how quickly it can all go away."

"It doesn't look like you've let your body go," Jacob said appreciatively and she flushed.

"I'll never dance professionally," she said. "I had to give up that dream. But it's impossible to go from working out forty hours a week to regular school and a desk job without including a good gym routine. I couldn't let myself lose all that strength and endurance. I was too good."

"So you're in great shape?" he teased. "In addition to being super modest?"

"I was a ballet dancer my whole life," she snapped, and he grinned at her fiery tone. "You can't imagine how grueling ballet really is. The ballerinas look airy and beautiful but it's all sweat and bloodied toes behind stage."

"Pretty tough," he said and she detected a note of condescension.

"Ballet dancers are the toughest athletes on earth," she fired at him.

Jacob threw up his hands. "When Baryshnikov wins the Tour de France, then you can talk to me about it," he said.

"That's ridiculous," Ariel sputtered, heat blooming on her cheeks, until she saw, once again, the twinkle in Jacob's eyes. When would she learn that his arrogance was mostly a show? Was part of his reputation for cockiness due to people being too intimidated, too unperceptive, to see that he was kidding around?

"I think we need some beers to settle this debate," said Jacob, sliding out of his seat. "I'll be right back."

Ariel watched him move over to the bar. So far all she'd done was talk about herself! He was too skilled at deflecting conversation away from anything revealing about his own life. He was still an enigma.

"Hi Red," came a deep voice. A man stood at her table, leering down at her. "Mind if I join you?" Ariel smiled briefly.

"No thanks," she said. "My friend will be right back."

"Your *friend*?" the man asked. He was none too steady on his feet. Ariel pointed at Jacob, who was striding toward them with two bottles of beer.

"Evening," said Jacob with a curt nod at the man. He slid a bottle across the table to Ariel.

"You wouldn't mind if I took this lovely lady for a spin on the dance floor, would you?" the man asked Jacob. "I mean, seeing as how you're just friends?"

Jacob sat down next to Ariel and threw an arm around her shoulder. He held the man's eye for a long moment. The tension between them crackled.

"As a matter of fact, I *would* mind," said Jacob slowly. "My friend and I have just decided to take our relationship to the next phase. So if you'll excuse us . . . " And with that, Jacob pulled Ariel against him. And he kissed her.

His lips were warm. Demanding. His tongue parted her lips and Ariel felt flames lick up her spine. Her surprised resistance melted in an instant and she responded to his kiss. She forgot about everything around her. With her eyes closed and Jacob's mouth claiming hers, she almost thought she was on the rooftop again, the stars close above her, a stranger's strong body cradling her, holding her close. She forgot it was Jacob she was kissing. Forgot everything but the feeling. The desire. From a great distance, it seemed, she heard the man mutter, "I get the point."

She broke away from Jacob and saw the man pushing his way toward the pool tables. She looked at Jacob. He'd leaned back against the booth. He was watching her closely. Waiting for her reaction. She flushed.

"What was *that* about?" she asked unsteadily.

"I could have told him to take the next dance," said Jacob. His voice was frankly unapologetic. "I could have said we weren't even friends. That you were a reporter and you'd be free as soon as we finished our business."

"Or you could have let me handle it myself," said Ariel. "Instead of acting out your machismo."

"Machismo?" Jacob repeated. "Hmmmm . . . " He folded his muscular arms across his chest. It looked like he was trying to fight back a smile. "Are you going to press with that?" he asked. "It's not the most original line . . . "

"What you just did was completely inappropriate," she said in a prim tone. She tried to scoot away from him but he closed the distance between them. There was no more room between her and the wall. His stared at her, eyes lingering on her lips. She couldn't fight the magnetic force that drew them together. But she tried.

"It was completely unprofessional," she continued. He dropped his head so that his lips were beside her ear.

"You didn't mind the other night," he whispered. Ariel's world spun. The whisper tickled her ear. Raised goose-bumps along her arms. "When I held you in my arms . . . in the light of the Milky Way . . . "

Ariel drew a shuddering breath. Jacob took her hand and gently pressed something into her palm. She looked down. A golden charm.

"You lost this," said Jacob gently. "It seems like it may be important to you."

"It is," Ariel whispered. "It's very important to me." She slipped the charm into her pocket. She hadn't even noticed it was gone. The thought of losing it made her breath catch in her throat. How could she reconcile this moody man, the subject of her investigation, with the man on the rooftop who took her breath away? Who flooded her with passion? She'd almost had sex with him even though she'd only met him moments before. Even though she hadn't known his name. But if she admitted to herself, she must have realized it was him.

Jacob Hunter.

She wanted to kill him. She wanted to kiss him. She let him to lead her back to the parking lot. She slid behind him onto the motorcycle in silence.

The wind felt cool and soothing, but it wasn't enough. Her body was on fire everywhere it came into contact with Jacob's. She was aching, burning with desire for him. When he pulled up outside the hotel, she jumped off the bike, breaking the physical contact between them as quickly as she could.

She had never felt so confused in her life. How could she reconcile her feelings for this man with the demands of her assignment? And if she couldn't handle this assignment professionally, objectively, and ethically—meaning *not* sleeping with her subject—what did it say about her as a journalist? She'd already lost one career to a weakness of the body. She wasn't losing a second.

She followed Jacob to the elevators without speaking, her thoughts in a whirl. They entered the same elevator and Jacob pushed the button for his floor.

"Ariel . . . " began Jacob as the door slid closed. He pulled her against him for a deep kiss. A kiss that turned her legs to jelly. She felt his hands move down her back, cup her bottom. He held her tightly so that her belly nestled against his rock-hard thighs.

She took a deep breath. Stepped back from him. She pushed the button for her own floor, below Jacob's.

"Jacob," she said in a tight, high voice, "why don't you tell me about the bar fight you had in Minturn last week?"

Jacob stared at her, emotions playing across his face. Surprise. Anger. Even—hurt? Ariel was suddenly overcome with despair.

"Why are you asking me that?" he said softly.

"Because I'm here to write a story about you," said Ariel, miserably. "Remember? I'm not here for . . . *this*."

Jacob's handsome face grew hard. "There is no *this*," he said. They stared at each other for a long moment in silence.

The door opened at Ariel's floor. She bolted from the elevator, hot tears spilling onto her cheeks. The sound of Jacob's voice followed her down the hall.

"If you have trouble sleeping, try to stay out of the pool. That's where the sharks hang out."

Ariel flung herself on her bed. She'd have no problem staying away from the pool tonight. No problem at all.

Chapter Seven

The sun rose over the crest of Red Peak, sending exploratory rays through the cracks in Ariel's curtains. Ariel woke at the first touch of the sun's light on her face. For a moment, she lay comfortably in the warm, soft nest of the hotel bed, enjoying the silky feel of the high thread count sheets and the plump down pillows.

Her comfort was short-lived. As soon as her sleep-fogged mind cleared enough to bring the events of the previous night into focus, she sat bolt upright, her heart pounding. What had she done? Jeopardized—no, ruined—her chances at writing a serious story on Jacob Hunter. She'd broken all the rules of journalistic ethics, gotten too involved—far, far too involved—with her subject . . . with Jacob. The man she was supposed to be investigating.

She had failed miserably. She didn't even know if she could face Jacob again.

She sprang out of bed, the wild idea of packing and getting on the first plane back to New York half-formed in her mind. Still in her pajamas, she dragged her suitcase from the closet and began gathering her clothing from the dresser where she'd neatly placed it just a few days before.

Just as she'd finished collecting her underthings into a tidy bundle, there was a knock on the door. Confused—the maids didn't start cleaning rooms this early—Ariel yelled, "Just a minute!"

Grabbing a terry cotton robe from a hook in the bathroom, she opened the door to find a young man in the white shirt and black vest of the hotel restaurant staff. He was pushing a cart covered in immaculate white linen, set with silver dishes and pitchers, graced with a bouquet of beautiful blue flowers in a crystal vase. As if reading her mind, the young man nodded toward the flowers as he wheeled the cart to a spot near the window. "Colorado Rocky Mountain Columbine. Special request. The florists don't have them. Wonder who had to scamper all over the mountains for those?" He grinned at Ariel.

Since when are teenagers so cheerful at seven in the morning? Ariel wondered. Removing the lids from the dishes to reveal baskets of croissants and muffins as well as a plate of scrambled eggs, bacon, toast, and hash browns, he said, "Guy who ordered it said you'd be needing a good breakfast. Said to give you this." He handed her a shopping bag from one of the town's nicer boutiques, concealed on the lower rack of the cart.

"Café au lait?" he asked brightly, unfazed by Ariel's startled expression. He took her silence for assent, and poured her a cup of coffee, mixing it half and half with hot milk till it turned a creamy, light brown.

It smelled delicious—Ariel was suddenly dying for a cup of that perfectly roasted coffee. Her teenage waiter turned to go. Ariel fumbled for her purse. "Don't worry ," he said with another cocky grin, "he already took care of the tip."

Ariel could guess who "he" might be. She sighed and sat down to breakfast.

By the time, she'd finished her food—as much of it as she could eat—and drunk nearly the whole pot of coffee, Ariel was thinking more clearly. It would be crazy, she told herself, to run away at a time like this, just when things were getting interesting.

Remembering the mysterious bag, she sat down on the bed and opened it to find not, as she'd expected, some tourist gewgaw, but what looked like a complete set of cycling gear. Exactly what Jacob wore. Shorts, jersey, gloves, socks, shoes. All in sizes far smaller than Jacob would have fit into.

At the bottom of the bag, there was an envelope. Ariel extracted a notecard—heavy stock embossed with the hotel's name and crest. In angular, masculine handwriting, the note read, *I'm sorry for what happened last night. I'd like to spend the day with you. You said your readers wanted to know Jacob Hunter, the man, that they already know Jacob Hunter, the athlete. But to know the man, you have to know the sport. Get ready for your ride.*

Ariel sat down on the bed, completely taken aback. She was surprised that Jacob had apologized for what had happened between them. Hadn't she been the one to upset him, bringing up the fight in the bar? Then to run away from the intensity of their openly expressed physical attraction? She had a hard time imagining that Jacob was perceptive enough to understand that it was exactly that intensity that had led to her outburst, her conflicted feelings for him causing her to lash out just when they'd acknowledged that they wanted each other . . . badly. But, since the moment they'd met, Jacob had done nothing but surprise her.

She flushed, remembering the feeling of his rock-hard body supporting her own, of pressing herself against him shamelessly, of melting into his kiss. Feeling the sudden ache of desire deep in her belly, she wondered again how she would face him this morning.

It was clear, however, that running away was no longer an option. She had to finish what she'd started. She could let this story derail her career, cost her her future—or she could continue to delve into the mystery of Jacob's behavior, and publish whatever she discovered. A real breakthrough on this story could make her very, very successful.

As soon as she had the thought, Ariel was awash with guilt. She couldn't understand why, though. At least not intellectually. Wasn't Jacob a hotshot athlete cheating to win? A macho egomaniac? But then he did such surprisingly kind things. Like send her breakfast. With flowers.

Ariel had to face facts. Her fascination with Jacob was more than professional. She was consumed with the desire to understand his contradictory signals, to learn his secrets. It was clear he had secrets. Maybe it was just the coffee talking, but she was for the first time completely confident in her ability to learn them all. But what, she wondered, would she do once she had?

Jumping up from the bed, Ariel showered and then set herself to the task of dressing herself in the unfamiliar clothing Jacob had sent her. It wasn't complicated. But when she finished, she wondered if she'd have the nerve to leave her room in anything so revealing.

Ariel wasn't unduly modest. But as she examined herself nervously in the full-length mirror, she had a hard time imagining that her outfit could be considered decent, by anyone. Excepting her time in dance studios and onstage, she'd never worn anything so . . . *tight*.

Both the shorts and the jersey were in Jacob's team colors—black, striped up the sides with burgundy and white, the sponsors name's printed in white on the chest, back, and shoulders. Craning her head over her shoulder, Ariel noted that the spandex was completely molded to her body, revealing every swell and contour of her waist, her legs—and her derriere. She sighed. Theo had no idea what he'd gotten her into. She was going to kill him. Just as soon as she made it back to New York.

She looked around the room, wondering if she needed anything else. She'd have to assume that Jacob had it covered. Marshaling her courage, she left the room and let the lock click behind her—wondering, in the meantime, where she was supposed to put her key-card.

In the elevator, she patted herself down for pockets, discovering one at the small of her back. She slipped the card into it and waited for the elevator to ding at Jacob's floor. As the door slid open, she threw her shoulders back and shook her damp hair out behind her. If she'd learned anything in her time as a dancer, it was that perfect posture was often an adequate substitute for real confidence.

Marching down the hall to Jacob's door, she forced herself to knock immediately and loudly. Revealing her underlying timidity wasn't going to get her anywhere. Jacob answered the door more quickly than Ariel would have liked. He was dressed in identical spandex, and as soon as he saw her a raffish grin lit up his handsome face.

"You look great," he told her, raking her up and down with hungry eyes. Did he find her attractive in her bizarre get-up? Ariel was incredulous. But there was no mistaking the gleam in his eyes. Or the sudden tumescence in his shorts.

*

Stepping back from the door, Jacob intentionally held it open so that she passed in front of him into the room, hungrily appreciating the swelling curves of her ass cupped in black spandex. It was just as spectacular as he'd expected. Truth be told, he'd been looking forward to this moment all morning. And with the day he'd planned ahead of them, he'd be enjoying the sight of it for hours longer.

He was amazed by the intensity of his sudden desire to press his groin against the succulent roundness of her backside, to feel his hard manhood cradled by the cleft of her buttocks, to slip himself into the sweet, slick heaven between her legs.

Easy, boy, he told himself, *you don't want to spend the whole day with a hard-on for all the world to see. Think of baseball.*

Turning to face him, Ariel said, "So we're going on a ride? Don't you have to train today? I might slow you up."

"Today's an easy day. I'm resting this week. Today I'm scheduled to do seventy miles. Easy pace. It'll be no problem for an athlete like yourself," he said challengingly.

But all she said was, "Sounds great. I'd love to see more of the countryside. The mountains are so beautiful. Where will we be riding?"

"We'll have the van drop us on a loop road, up in one of the ski bowls. Pretty flat—relatively speaking. I've got everything we need in the van. Including a bike for you."

He ushered her out the door—feasting his eyes on her ravishing figure all the way down the hall.

*

They rode for several miles in companionable silence. Ariel was stunned by the beauty of the majestic mountains, the alpine meadows sprinkled with wildflowers, the rushing brooks. After a few hours, however, her legs began to burn, and her breath caught in her throat during the frequent climbs.

Just like spin class, she told herself. *Power through it.* She couldn't help wondering, with trepidation, how many miles they'd come—and how many more they had to go.

She was also certain that she was slowing Jacob's progress dramatically. His "easy" pace felt like a sprint to her. She could keep up with him on the flat stretches—barely—but she couldn't help falling behind as they made their way up long, gradual hills.

Ariel wasn't in top dancing form, but still, she walked everywhere in the city, went to the gym, and went to yoga and pilates when she could fit the classes into her week. She was in pretty good shape. But the altitude wore on her more than she expected. They were at least nine thousand feet above sea level. The air was clear, clean—and thin. Ariel gasped and panted. She was annoyed that she wasn't making the tough, strong impression she'd wanted to make on Jacob. After a few more miles, however, she was too wiped out to focus on feeling annoyed. Or to focus on anything else besides the pavement slipping away under her wheels.

He'd told her to ride slightly behind and to the side of him, drafting in his wake. She was grateful for his easy silence and his obvious concessions to her inexperience. After they'd ridden for what felt like hours—Jacob pausing only for Ariel to catch up at the tops of the increasingly painful hills, and to sip water from her sports bottle—Ariel heard a sudden sharp crack, followed by a loud rattling. She felt a jolt and then a sudden slackness in her peddling. She coasted to an involuntary stop, looking down to see what the problem was. It seemed her chain had broken. It hung sadly from the teeth of her chain ring.

Jacob stopped beside her, frowning with displeasure. "Goddamn Ben," he swore, an angry look on his face. "I told him to have the mechanics look that bike over this morning. It should be in perfect condition." He looked up at her, and for a moment, Ariel thought she saw a speculative expression flit across his features. Then he simply looked annoyed. She felt too tired to try to analyze his reaction, simply grateful for the rest this technical problem was providing.

"Can you fix it?" she asked. She was annoyed to hear the fatigue in her voice. *Man up, Ariel,* she told herself. *Isn't this the moment when you show this guy how tough you are?*

"No," Jacob shook his head emphatically. "I don't have the tools." He turned to scan the landscape around them. They'd come to a stop in a little ravine, with rises on each side crested by fir trees. Ariel thought she heard the chattering of a brook nearby. "We'll have to hang out for a little bit. We can eat some energy bars and rest up. When we don't show up on time, the van will come looking for us. Shouldn't be too long." He gestured up the hill to the trees. "We'll leave the bikes up there so they see us. I think there's a creek on the other side. Nice and shady. Come on up."

Dismounting their bikes, they carried them up the little hill on their shoulders, resting them against a tree at the top, in full view of the road. Sure enough, a charming brook babbled in the decline on the other side of the hill. Its grassy banks were dotted with the same flowers Jacob had sent her with breakfast. Stands of firs offered cool shade.

Descending to the bank of the stream, Ariel was again able to appreciate the beauty of the scenery. She arched her back, relishing the restorative stretch, as well as the crystalline, fir-scented air and the clarity of the water as it ran over its bed of polished stones. She sank appreciatively onto the soft grass and folded herself over her legs to stretch her sore hamstrings.

*

She looked even more beautiful in this perfect natural setting, thought Jacob, than she had at the hotel. He marveled at her flexibility as she spread her legs out straight to the sides in a perfect split and lowered her upper body until it was flat against the ground. What options could that flexibility offer them in bed?

He sat down beside her, lounging easily on his elbows and handing her a power bar. Ariel bit into it hungrily, then looked at the bar's label.

"That's one of the perks of working out this hard. You can eat as many calories as you want, whenever. I have trouble keeping my weight up, not down," Jacob offered conversationally.

Ariel nodded. "I don't worry about it, either. When I was dancing, all the other girls were starving themselves to look like 'perfect' ballerinas. But they were so undernourished, they had no energy for the actual dancing. Long hours, hard work. You need food for that. I concentrated on technique, on fitness, on stamina—and let my weight take care of itself."

Jacob ran his eyes over her body appreciatively. "It seems to be taking care of itself quite nicely, still."

Ariel blushed. She jumped up and crossed the few feet between their resting place and the bank of the stream, where she knelt and splashed her face with water.

As she straightened up, Jacob also rose. Before Ariel could turn around, he grasped her from behind, pressing the length of their bodies together, front to back. Just as he'd imagined.

Ariel gasped as Jacob pulled her against him, one hand on her right breast and the other wrapped around her waist. Her whole body melted against him, and he took her weight effortlessly. Her head fell back against his shoulder and he kissed her neck hungrily, tasting the salt of her sweat. He felt the delicious weight of Ariel's breast filling his palm, the firm ripeness of her bottom. He pressed himself more tightly into her, his penis rock-hard under the spandex of his shorts. He moved his other hand lower, toward the triangle of Ariel's sex.

*

As Ariel felt Jacob's hand on her, pressing against her clitoris through the thin fabric of her clothes, she let out a low, involuntary moan.

She wanted this man. Wanted him more than she'd wanted anyone, ever. The intensity of her desire was overwhelming. It pulsed in hot waves from between her legs, half pleasure, half ache. She opened her legs for his hand, allowing him to spread his palm between her thighs, to move it against the slippery fabric, over the locus of her mounting pleasure.

She moaned when he took his hand away—then moaned again, more loudly, as he slipped his hand down her shorts, touching her again with no intervening fabric to dull the incredible sensation. Jacob groaned as his fingers slid against the slick folds of her sex, circling her tender, swollen bud with lazy, teasing fingers.

He picked her up entirely and, turning her to face him, lowered her onto the soft grass beside the stream. Covering her body with his own, he pushed her willing legs open, rested his hips between them and moved against her, the slow friction driving Ariel to delirium.

They stripped one another's clothes off in a frenzy, Jacob kissing every part of Ariel's skin as he uncovered it. Ariel felt she was afloat in a sea of sensation, her rational mind entirely drowned in a rising, rushing tide of desire. When Jacob lowered his head between her legs and moved his tongue expertly against her clit, she shuddered with amazement, all her senses aflame, her body rocking as waves of pleasure spread from her core through every part of her being.

Feeling her pleasure mount—with shocking quickness—toward the crest of climax, she curled her fingers under his jaw and pulled his head up toward her own, kissing his slick mouth, drowning in the depths of his kiss. All her inhibitions knocked asunder by her maddening need for the feeling of his manhood inside her, filling her completely, she whispered into his ear, "I want you . . . now."

Jacob lifted himself above her, looking down at her. Like her, he was breathing quickly, excited, flushed. To Ariel's complete shock, and her intense frustration, he shook his head. "I don't have a condom," he whispered, stroking the side of her face gently, regretfully.

Ariel couldn't fathom his restraint. There was no way they could not make love now. It was destiny, fate. It was primal, a deep, instinctive need. It was more necessary than anything she'd ever felt. She raised her head and kissed him deeply, pressing her hips against him at the same time.

"It doesn't matter," she said, gazing up at him with complete trust, complete hedonistic abandon, running her hands up and down his smooth back.

Jacob pulled farther away from her, separating their bodies by a few inches. Ariel never knew a few inches could matter so much. Hurt so much. Almost sobbing with frustration, she begged him, "Please. I need you. I want you, now. I don't care about the condom."

Jacob kissed her forehead and stroked her hair, gazing at her compassionately, the fire of passion still in his eyes. "I know," he said. "I know, love. I want it as much as you do. But I do care. For both of us. We'll have to wait until later."

Ariel pulled herself away from him entirely, rocketing to her feet and looking at him as he lay below her in the grass. Incredibly beautiful. All she wanted in the world, at this moment. To her intense shame and surprise, she broke into a torrent of tears.

Covering her face with her hands, she turned away from Jacob, stumbling down the bank of the stream. She wanted to hide herself, hide her frustration, her embarrassment. Because, as the heat of her lust faded, she knew Jacob was right. She'd just pressed him to behave incredibly irresponsibly, had urged him to put both of them at risk. She dropped her hands and walked quickly down the bank, looking for a place to collect herself, to calm the turmoil of her emotions—alone. Passing through the stand of firs, she rounded the face of a giant rock and sat down in the grass naked, her back pressed against the warm stone, taking deep, restorative breaths. She was hidden from Jacob. Just as she'd wanted.

*

Allowing her to pass out of sight, Jacob rose and followed her at a distance, treading lightly with his bare feet on the sward of grass. He saw her slip behind the rock, and, not seeing her emerge, stood a moment in indecision. Should he follow her? No, he decided. He'd seen the desperation in her eyes, the crazy jumble of her thoughts and feelings. Intuitively, he felt that she needed this time alone, that he should respect her privacy—for a while.

*

When Ariel came out from behind her rock, she thought she'd figured a few things out. Jacob Hunter was a more respectful, gentle, selfless person than she ever could have expected. And she herself was capable of things she'd never imagined—risking everything for a moment of fleeting—albeit incredibly intense—pleasure, letting her body completely rule her mind, her good judgment.

She was embarrassed. But she was also interested in this new version of Ariel Hayes. Was it so bad to prioritize pleasure? Maybe she had some unexpected exploration ahead of her.

She glanced around for Jacob. He was nowhere in sight. She returned to where her clothes lay, huddled on the ground beside the stream, and dressed herself. She wasn't entirely eager to face Jacob again. He'd seen a side of her she never knew she had. Seen her in the throes of raw, aching abandon. She'd lost all her defenses—and she wasn't sure if she could rebuild them.

Jacob came bounding down the hill from the direction of the road, looking infuriatingly good-humored and casual. "Hey," he said gently, approaching her more slowly and tucking a strand of hair behind her ear. "I fixed the bike. We can get going. Only another fifteen miles or so to the pick-up point."

"You fixed the bike?" Ariel asked incredulously. "I thought you said you couldn't fix the bike."

"I lied. I thought you could use a rest. It's an easy fix, actually, as long as you have a chain breaker with you. I always carry one." He grinned at her roguishly—and then had the gall to actually wink.

Ariel was flabbergasted—and furious. How dare he trick her like this, see her weakness and lie to her to indulge it? Had he planned that scene on the grass?

"That was inexcusable," she told him icily. "I can't stand dishonesty." She stalked up the hill, grabbed the repaired bicycle, and started up the road without waiting for Jacob.

The remainder of their ride was conducted in silence. Ariel

was too angry to notice the discomfort of her aching legs, her sore back. They made it back to the van without a hitch. Ariel didn't speak to Jacob as they drove back to the hotel. They separated in the lobby, Ariel intentionally allowing Jacob to take the first elevator alone so she wouldn't have to share it with him.

It was only when she was back in her room, stripping the spandex off her aching body, that Ariel cooled down enough to recognize how hypocritical she was being. She'd told Jacob that she couldn't stand dishonesty. But she was pretending to be someone she wasn't in order to trick him into revealing his potentially incriminating secrets.

What a total mess, she thought, collapsing on her bed.

Chapter Eight

"I don't know if cyclists take drugs, Theo," Ariel said, wincing as she paced the carpet. "They might just be intensely masochistic." Every muscle in Ariel's body was screaming. She could barely walk. Jacob's "easy" ride had nearly killed her. And had completely destroyed her self-respect.

Not that she'd told Theo about *that*. Her ears grew hot just thinking about it. Jacob had driven her out of her senses. She'd been utterly shameless. She'd been willing to sacrifice everything in the heat of the moment—her journalistic integrity, the story, her career.

What if Jacob hadn't stopped? What if she'd gotten pregnant? An icy wave of panic coursed through her, followed by images of golden haired babies with golden eyes, their golden-eyed father standing over them, looking down at them with that unbelievably intense expression. An expression of absolute concentration. Devotion. Love.

"Fascinating," Theo was saying drily. Ariel could hear the sounds of traffic in the background and knew that Theo must be walking back to the office with his daily iced caramel macchiato, tall, non-fat milk.

"*X-Ray* is going to break a story about mental illness in professional cycling. Good work, Ariel. You're ready for *The Dr. Oz Show*. Jacob Hunter can get live therapy with shrinks in the studio audience."

Ariel groaned. "Theo, I'm kidding. It's not that I think Jacob's clean. It's just that I'm starting to understand how hard he rides. How good he really is. I think maybe he just doesn't respond to pain like a regular person."

Or else maybe he likes pain, she thought. Yesterday he'd pulled back from the brink of an unbelievably sensual experience. When their bodies separated, Ariel had felt it as keenly as a blow. But maybe the feeling was less powerful for him? She fell back onto the bed and her body protested. Loudly.

"Bottom line," Theo said as a car horn blared. "Drug abuse is *the* major issue in sports. Sure, masochism may be relevant. You could maybe make Jacob Hunter's masochism into a human-interest piece. A one-column article. But, Ariel, this is your opportunity to write a feature story with serious merit and mass appeal. In the world of journalism, merit and mass appeal means hard-hitting *scandal.* The scandal is there. Find it." The phone muffled briefly and Ariel heard Theo shouting.

"Goddamn gypsy cabs," he muttered. "So listen, darling, as I was saying. Illegal drugs, yes. Jacob Hunter's use of visualization techniques to control pre-race anxiety, no. Get it? Do you see the difference?"

"I see it," Ariel responded.

"Good." Theo's voice sounded peppier, clearer, and Ariel knew that he'd entered the lobby of the office building. "I read an article the other day about Hunter having a bar fight with some local tough."

"I'm on that already, Theo," said Ariel. "Brian Jenks. He lives in Leadville."

"That's what I read the other day," said Theo. "What I read the other day is, as we call it in this profession, *old news.* Have you found out anything new? Have you talked to Brian Jenks?"

"Not yet," Ariel admitted. "I found his home number in the phone book. I was going to call him today."

"Then why are we still on the phone, my dear?" said Theo brightly. "You're finally making sense. Now go make sense out of Brian Jenks."

At the abrupt sound of the dial tone, Ariel let her phone drop out of her hand. She should have known she was due for a lashing from Theo. After all, she'd been ignoring all his calls and hadn't been sending email updates.

"He's right," she said aloud. She'd been avoiding the hard issues. She hadn't really been digging to find out about drug use. Why was that? The answer came swiftly. Unbidden.

She didn't want to believe it was true. Didn't want to believe that Jacob was living a lie. She'd gone into this thing wanting to take him down a peg. Now she had to admit she was falling under his spell. Starting to believe the myth. It was hard not to believe it when you saw him ride. The grace. The power. She remembered Steve Fratello's words. *He's the best the sport has to offer.* She couldn't help but want to believe that Jacob's talent and passion made him the best. That he had something you couldn't find in a syringe.

Well that attitude wasn't going to win her a Pulitzer. At this rate, it might even get her fired. She fumbled for her phone and notebook. Without another moment's hesitation, she found the number she was looking for and dialed. The phone rang and rang and rang again. Just as she was about to give up, she heard a click.

"What do you want?" came a gruff male voice.

"Hello," she said. "Brian Jenks?"

*

Jacob stood in the hotel lobby. He'd left his room almost an hour ago but hadn't managed to make up his mind as to where to go. He'd walked out of the elevator and just stopped.

He wasn't sure what to do with himself. It was a strange feeling. Usually, he had something on his plate. A training ride. A morale-building lunch with the guys. *Something.* Today loomed empty in front of him. Empty because . . . Well, because he knew what he wanted to be doing. He wanted to get back in the elevator and punch Ariel's floor number. He wanted to show up at her door with a bouquet of columbines and a box of condoms and finish what he'd started. He wanted to slide into her and feel her clamping around him. Her thighs clutching him. He wanted to hear her moan again with that wild abandon.

To be honest, he hadn't expected it. Even after the night in the pool, he hadn't really believed that Ariel Hayes, that prickly reporter, could let herself go so magnificently, so enticingly. It was driving him mad. It was all he could think about.

His cell rang and he declined a call from Liz. The fourth of the day. He raked his hands through his hair. Guilt and irritation. He had to get out of this indecisive funk. There was one thing he should be doing with his free afternoon, but he wasn't sure he was up to it. Visiting hours were two p.m. to five p.m. His reluctance to get on his motorcycle and make the short trip made him feel awful. But it would make him feel worse to go and find what he didn't want to find . . .

He *had* to stop hovering in the hotel lobby. The artificial light made him feel agitated. He loved being outdoors. Even if he wasn't going cycling or getting on his motorcycle, he could at least take a walk around Vail Village.

But then he'd be less likely to run into Ariel.

He should go to visiting hours. That's what he should do. He scrolled through the numbers on his phone. He'd call the hospital first. Let her know he was coming.

Suddenly, he realized that he'd been zoning out, staring at the elevator. The doors opened and his teammates Steve and Randall walked toward him.

"Jakey," said Steve, grinning. "You turning into a lounge lizard? I'm going to have to tell Coach that you don't know what to do with yourself on relaxation days. Ben said he saw you in the lobby an hour ago."

"We're going out for avocado shakes," said Randall. "Want to join us for a fat blast?"

Jacob tried to return their friendly smiles.

"I had a salmon-avocado wrap for breakfast," he said. "I might be done with avocadoes for the day."

"So that's your secret?" Steve laughed, and Jacob jerked slightly. He pressed his phone screen-down into his thigh in a quick, involuntary motion. Then he took a deep breath as Steve kept talking. "Everyone wants to know how you blaze those hills. Salmon-avocado breakfast wraps. Not the sexiest answer. But good for the wrap industry."

"I do endorse the wrap industry," said Jacob. Had his teammates noticed his strange reaction to the word "secret"? It didn't seem like it. They seemed as unrattled and friendly as ever. "I've been holding out on you gentlemen," continued Jacob. "I also add cheese."

"Salmon-avocado-cheese wraps. You should write a cookbook, Jakey," said Steve.

"Are you looking forward to the party tonight?" asked Randall.

Dammit. So that's what Liz had been calling about. He'd completely forgotten. He knew it was ridiculous to say aloud, but he was tired of the sponsors' lavish meet-and-greet parties. He was tired of all of it: the champagne, the canapés, the boring conversations, the adoring but vapid ski bunnies and corporate wives.

He imagined pulling Ariel into a dark corner of the posh restaurant. Feeding her prosciutto and melon from a silver tray. Well, *that* didn't seem too bad. But add about two hundred other people into the mix and things turned kind of ugly. Especially if fifty of them were reporters and one of them was Liz.

Ariel was a reporter, he reminded himself. That cautionary line seemed weaker every time. He couldn't seem to bring himself to avoid her. He couldn't even keep his hands off her. He'd resigned himself to that. He'd just have to be careful not to reveal too much. While at the same time revealing all of her . . . her gorgeous curves . . . to his hungry gaze.

It didn't seem fair. But then, life wasn't fair. He'd learned that lesson early when his father's vision deteriorated and he'd had to stop driving trucks, the family eking along on his disability and his mother's small salary as a school nurse.

Thinking about his family caused Jacob's stomach to tighten. He had to get out of the hotel lobby.

"I'll see you guys tonight," he said to his friends. "I'm taking the motorcycle out for a spin."

"Addicted to speed," sighed Steve. "It's a burden, we know." He punched Jacob lightly in the stomach.

"See you later, dude."

When Jacob pulled out on his motorcycle minutes later, he looked all around before turning toward the highway. He didn't want anyone to know what direction he rode. He opened the throttle and shot out of Vail like a rocket.

*

When Ariel finally decided she felt mobile enough to grab some lunch, she went out into Vail Village and ran into Steve Fratello and Randall Henderson.

"Hi there," Steve called to her in that same cheerful tone she remembered from their last interaction. "Want a sip?"

"Spirulina smoothie?" guessed Ariel, inspecting the tall, clear plastic cup that Steve held out to her.

"Avocado shake," said Steve. "Have as much you want. It's my second."

"Your *second*?" asked Ariel. Cyclists certainly loved to eat. What would Theo think if instead of drugs she wrote that Jacob Hunter was using avocadoes? The thought made her smile. "You guys don't worry about calories," she said, remembering Jacob's speech the day before.

"I worry about not getting enough," said Randall with a serious look on his face.

"Careful," said Steve. "This guy's a wolf. He's been known to go for the arms of other guys riding in his pack."

"Not after a few avocado shakes," said Randall. "You're safe for now."

Ariel's smile widened. At first, she'd taken Randall to be stiffer and less quirky than Steve Fratello, but it seemed he had a sense of humor in his own right.

"You're safe, too," said Ariel. "I just treated myself to sashimi."

"Girl can eat," said Steve approvingly. "I don't know what you're talking about exactly, but it sounds good."

Ariel nodded. Then, in case the men already knew, she decided not to beat around the bush. "I went on a bike ride with Jacob yesterday," she said casually. "I needed to replenish myself. I knew when I left the hotel that a soup and salad wasn't going to cut it."

When Ariel saw Steve and Randall exchange glances, she knew that Jacob hadn't said anything about their ride. She wasn't sure if she felt grateful or annoyed. Maybe Jacob took women cycling all the time. In Milan. In Paris. Maybe women were always breaking their chains, abandoning their bicycles, and begging him to make love to them. Mortification caused Ariel's face to flame anew.

"You must be in pretty good shape to ride with Jake," observed Randall.

"We weren't exactly sprinting," said Ariel, but Randall was shaking his head.

"Still," he said. "We are in the Rocky Mountains. In case you haven't noticed."

"It was a little hilly." Ariel laughed with a rush of pride. "I wouldn't want to do it again today. Maybe tomorrow though."

Steve and Randall were looking at her with respect.

"I like your attitude, Hayes," said Steve. "I bet Jacob does, too."

What did he mean by that? Ariel scanned his face for a hint of irony or insinuation but failed to find anything behind that frank open grin.

"Why don't you come to the party tonight at Il Terrazo?" suggested Randall. "Our sponsors like to throw parties for promotion. Lots of free food and drink. It's a good way of making sure that nobody eats any arms."

"I'll be there," said Ariel, surprised at the real warmth she heard in her voice.

So far, cyclists were *nicer* than she'd assumed they'd be. She almost felt like she was making friends.

*

The party at Il Terrazzo was shaping up to be everything Ariel had expected. The sponsors had rented out the entire restaurant. Inside, beautiful young waitresses drifted around from table to table with silver trays of sparkling drinks. Men in dark suits were leaning against the bar, talking seriously and waving heavy glasses of amber liquors.

Walking out onto the restaurant terrace and noting the spread of delicacies on the banquet tables, Ariel realized that Randall was right. Nobody would be eating any arms tonight.

If she were in New York, Ariel would have worn a classic little black dress to the restaurant party. Elegant. Safe. You couldn't go wrong. But here in Colorado, the fashion code was . . . more colorful. And Ariel had dressed accordingly. She'd worn a short, tight emerald green dress with a plunging back. It was a dress she'd packed at the last minute—almost unable to believe she was doing it—because she'd remembered Theo's admonition to have more fun. Well, the dress was definitely fun. She was afraid it was a little *too* fun. But it was too late now. She felt daring in the dress, if over-exposed.

Ariel shook her curls out of her face and walked toward the banquet tables, aware that people were turning to look at her. She tried not to search for Jacob among the young, good-looking men clustered along the stone balustrade. She hoped she didn't trip on the way to the table. As a dancer, Ariel knew she could summon a certain amount of grace. But not after she'd turned her muscles to jelly with that "easy" bike ride. She felt like she was wobbling with every step.

Breathe, Ariel told herself. *You're not running a gauntlet. You're going to get a plate of shrimp cocktail.*

                   *

Jacob saw Ariel the instant she stepped onto the terrace. It was as though he'd been caught in a tractor beam. He couldn't help but gawk over Liz's shoulder. Ariel's curves were hugged by the brilliantly colored fabric that set off her gorgeous green eyes to perfection. She'd left her bright hair down in a mass of riotous curls, pulled back from her face here and there by bobby pins.

Everyone on the terrace had stopped conversing to stare at her. Everyone except Liz who kept talking, her back to Ariel. Until she noticed that Jacob wasn't paying her the slightest bit of attention. Liz turned and when she saw the voluptuous redhead moving toward the banquet table, her jaw dropped. Not in a good way.

Jacob wanted to be polite. He didn't want to be rude to Liz, who, let's face it, was an energetic, attractive, wonderful woman. But he could barely form the words to excuse himself. Every fiber of his being was pulled toward Ariel and he didn't look at Liz as he found himself walking to intercept Ariel at the banquet table.

He reached her just as she was about to grab a piece of shrimp. Sensing his presence, she paused and looked up. When her green eyes hit him, he felt like he'd been struck by lightning. Unfortunately, a certain part of his anatomy was acting as a lightning rod. He wasn't sure how much of it he could take. He reached out and brushed her hand. She caught her lower lip between her teeth and he could tell that she was equally caught in the magnetic field that crackled between them.

Eyes never leaving hers, Jacob picked up a chilled pink shrimp and dipped it in cocktail sauce. He held it to her lips. Ariel's eyes began to shine. She took a bite of shrimp, lips curving in a smile. Jacob was staring at those lips. He had wanted this woman so badly. All last night. All day. Now she was standing in front of him and he couldn't wait any longer.

"You look good in spandex," said Jacob and Ariel's eyes flashed.

"This isn't spandex," she retorted and it was all he could do not to crush her in his arms. He ran his eyes over her, an eyebrow raised.

*

Ariel flushed, crossed her arms beneath her breasts. She was regaining awareness of her surroundings. What a spectacle she was making of herself! Letting Jacob Hunter hand-feed her shrimp at a crowded party!

She noticed the leggy blond she'd seen talking with Jacob in the hotel lobby glaring at her with unmitigated hatred. *Oh great,* thought Ariel as Jacob reached out and trailed his knuckles down the curve of her waist.

"The green is even better on you than my team colors," he said to her. Then he delivered a full, heart-stopping grin. "Ready for another ride?"

The sexual tension between them was palpable. Ariel wondered if it would start to melt the ice around the shrimp. She couldn't resist him.

"Are you challenging me, Jacob Hunter?" she asked, lifting her chin. Had he noticed how slowly she'd been walking? Her muscles still ached. The thought of another bicycle ride made her want to collapse. Of course, if she could manage to break her chain instantly . . . that might be the kind of ride she'd be ready for.

As if reading her thoughts, Jacob smiled, his handsome face filled with suggestion. "I'm challenging you, Ariel Hayes," he said. "Come with me. Right now. We have some unfinished business to attend to."

At the rich note in his voice, Ariel's legs almost buckled. She put her hand in Jacob's and let him pull her through the darkness of the restaurant and outside to the street.

It was already dark. The streetlight spilled over Jacob. His hair looked golden. Ariel couldn't help but stare at his firm ass in his tight dark jeans as he straddled his motorcycle. Would she regret this? Silly to even to wonder. She had no choice in the matter. She knew she'd follow Jacob Hunter wherever he wanted to go.

Ariel was surprised as they rode out of Vail Village and started climbing through the mountains. She swayed with Jacob as he leaned into the curves of the road. It was overwhelmingly sensual. Her body hugged his as the wind rushed past them and they rode endlessly on through the clear, fragrant night. At last, Jacob stopped the motorcycle on a long, desolate stretch of highway. On either side of them, the mountains rose majestically, silhouetted against the sky. Jacob climbed off the bike and his feet crunched on the road's gravel shoulder. Ariel came up close behind him.

She felt as though something strangely significant were about to happen. She had that same sense of mystery, of deep spiritual connection, that she'd experienced the first night in the pool . . . when Jacob was still a nameless stranger, a wanderer who pointed out the constellations.

The highway was utterly empty, running darkly into the distance. Why had Jacob brought her here? She heard the sounds of summer insects and the wind blowing through the spruce trees, carrying the scent of mountain flowers.

God, the air was so clean here in Colorado. The stars were so close.

Jacob turned toward her, cupped her face in his hands. She closed her eyes briefly and kissed his palm. Everything felt so right. She was so happy that they'd escaped the party, that they'd escaped from their social roles . . . the arrogant cyclist . . . the conniving reporter. Alone on this deserted road, they were simply Jacob and Ariel. Man and woman. Jacob broke the silence between them, his voice hoarse.

"My father used to take me here when I was a kid," he said. He put his arms around Ariel from behind, tucking his chin into her hair. The two of them stared down the highway together.

"They were still building this part of the highway," said Jacob. "This is an extension. It wasn't open for through-traffic. My father used to be a truck driver. He'd drive his rig on this road and I'd draft him on my bicycle. I'd never gone so fast. My father was pulling me behind him and it was like I could fly. Nothing can compare to that feeling. Afterwards, we'd drink thermoses of Mom's iced tea and sit on the side of the road just looking at the mountains."

"After my mother died, it was just me and my dad," whispered Ariel. "He worried about all the time I spent dancing. He wanted me to have something to fall back on. But he drove me to practice every day. He showed up to every recital. He taught high school English and he loved Shakespeare."

"That's how you got your name," said Jacob and when Ariel's body jolted slightly in surprise, he tightened his arms around her. "'The isle is full of noises,'" he quoted softly. "'Sounds and sweet airs, that give delight and hurt not.' It's from *The Tempest*. Ariel was a sprite. I paid attention in school, too," he said. "And I always loved English best. I still read a lot when I'm touring. Sometimes it feels like my books are the only things that stay constant as I go from country to country."

Ariel listened in amazement. Jacob was constantly surprising her. She turned in his arms and pressed herself into his chest. He claimed her lips and the sensation shivered over her. Running his hands over her bare arms, Jacob felt the goose-bumps on her skin. The mountain air had turned cold.

"My sprite," whispered Jacob, his lips burning on her neck. "Will you spend the night with me? If I promise you delight . . . "

Ariel's answer was muffled in his hungry kiss.

Chapter Nine

Jacob pulled Ariel through the door of the hotel suite, already sliding his hands up her short dress, pulling at the lacy panties beneath. Their mouths locked together, they grasped at one another feverishly.

Ariel tore at Jacob's belt, slipping the leather through the belt loops of his jeans and fumbling with the buttons beneath. Jacob lifted her in his strong arms and pinned her against the wall. He pulled the neck of her dress down from her shoulder, exposing her full breast, and lowered his mouth down on the tight bud of her nipple, circling it with his tongue, teasing and nipping at it with his teeth. Ariel cried out with pleasure.

She was crazed with desire for him. She'd waited for him long enough. She couldn't bear it. She hadn't felt like this about a man in . . . well, ever. She wanted to close up every particle of distance between their bodies. She needed him to press himself into her, to feel the full length of him penetrating her very core. Clutching at his shoulders, pulling his mouth up to kiss her again, she whispered in a ragged voice she didn't even recognize, "Now. Now."

And she looked into his eyes.

All the intensity and passion she'd seen in those eyes as he'd sprinted up the hill on his bicycle was now focused on her. She felt transfixed by that golden light. Skewered. She couldn't breathe.

Oh no, she thought, *what if I pass out?*

What if Jacob Hunter over-excited her so much that she ended up unconscious? That would be embarrassing. But she didn't need to worry. He was holding her completely, pressing her to the wall with his body. She couldn't collapse. She drew a shuddering breath and saw Jacob's eyes darken as he traced her lips with a fingertip.

He wanted her, too. It was written all over his face.

"Ariel," whispered Jacob and reached into his back pocket. He removed a condom and tore the package open with his teeth. The whole time his eyes held Ariel's; his gaze was mesmerizing, intoxicating. Ariel's panties were around her ankles and she kicked them off. Her skirt was up around her waist.

She couldn't believe what was happening. He ran his hand up her thigh, higher and higher, until he dipped his fingers into the wetness there. Moaning, she hooked her leg around his waist and he lifted her up.

Slowly, deliciously slowly, he eased his full length into her, pushing his hips against her. Her head fell forward. Her hair was in his face, in his mouth. Their sweaty foreheads banged together and Ariel laughed a rich, low laugh.

"Careful, Hunter," she said. "You're not wearing your helmet."

Chuckling, he held her even tighter against him, his hardness filling her completely. "Once I hit my head so hard I saw double," he said. "That doesn't sound so bad to me right now." He pushed her hair back with one hand. "The only thing more beautiful than you is two of you," he whispered.

"Shucks," Ariel whispered back, between kisses that made it hard for her speak. "You should be the writer . . . " She felt Jacob grin against her mouth.

Then his tongue was moving over her lips, sliding over her tongue. Their kiss grew deeper and deeper, and Ariel could no longer find words. Jacob began to move inside her. She met each thrust with a torque of her hips. He was so hard, so big. She dug her nails into his neck, forced his head down to her. She could hear his ragged breathing in her ear.

"I don't know how long I'll be able to stand you doing that . . . " he managed. Her next motion made him groan. She allowed herself a smile of pure triumph and moved her hips again. He cried out, his breath hot against her.

"Don't stop. Do it harder," she said. "This is the sprint. We have all night for the longer stages."

"Are you challenging me, Ariel Hayes?" Jacob panted.

"Show me what you've got," she said and rolled her hips until her own breath came in mewing cries.

He began to move against her more quickly, digging his hands into the silky flesh of her buttocks. Her head fell back and banged against the wall in rhythm with their movements. She didn't care. Each time he plunged into her she felt an explosion of sensation rocketing through her body. His slick shaft moved against her clitoris again and again.

Sooner than she would have thought possible, Ariel felt a mounting crest of heat rise through her and as it broke over her entirely she gasped again and again, coming harder than she ever had in her life. As she spasmed around him, Jacob followed her into climax, burying his face against her throat and forcing her hips down on him until they were both exhausted, slumping together in a tingling post-orgasmic glow.

Raising his head, still holding her, their bodies melded into one, he kissed her. His kiss was long, deep, slow.

"Hmmm . . . " said Ariel. She lifted a hand to rub the back of her head. "I think I was the one who needed a helmet."

She and Jacob let their foreheads touch, leaning into each other, laughing.

When had Ariel ever felt this comfortable with a man? Let alone with a man who'd just pushed her dress around her waist and ravished her against a wall? She had never felt so good. Her response was more than physical. Suddenly she realized that her connection to this man, her need for him, had to do with much more than her body. Her response to him was instinctive, rising from the deepest part of her. Overwhelming. Undeniable.

A part of her brain was still thinking clearly enough to find this alarming. *Not just sleeping with a subject. Falling in love with him.*

Then that part of her brain fell silent—extinguished by the languorous sweetness of Jacob's kiss, by the feeling of absolute comfort and safety she found within the circle of his arms, the desire for him that flickered, even now, like a flame coming to life, a flower blossoming.

"That was some sprint," Jacob murmured. "My best yet."

Twining her hands in his blond hair, she returned his kiss with a fullness, a generosity, a surrender that took both of them by surprise. Jacob's arms tightened around her. Still kissing her, he carried her to the bed and laid her gently down, her hair spread about her head like a blazing halo.

He sat on the side of the bed beside her and looked at her. Ariel felt that no one had ever looked at her like this before. That no one had ever, truly, seen her, in the way Jacob was seeing her now.

*

Slowly, gently, Jacob undressed her. Each part of her body that was revealed to him seemed more beautiful than the last. Finally, she lay before him entirely nude, reclining in complete relaxation, her half-lidded eyes meeting his fearlessly, un-self-consciously.

"Has anyone ever told you that you have a perfect body?" he asked.

"*Me?* Hardly," Ariel snorted. "Remember, I was a dancer. My body was always wrong. My neck was too short. My torso was too long. My thighs were too big. Even my hair was wrong. Can you imagine Clara in the Nutcracker with hair like Little Orphan Annie?"

"Wow." Jacob whistled. "Sounds like they did a number on you."

"I always took it with a grain of salt," said Ariel. "A dancer has to be more than an ideal body. I never wanted to be the plastic ballerina in the jewelry box. I tried to make being different work for me. Not having the traditional dancer's body just forced me to try harder. To dance with more energy. To take more risks. My mother used to tell me that I should never try to be someone different than who I was. I should just try to be my best self. And that self would be beautiful."

Jacob lay down beside her on the bed. He regarded her silently for a long moment, propped up on one elbow. Then he ran one fingertip from Ariel's delicate ear, down her graceful neck to the hollow between her collarbones. He continued to trace a line between the lush globes of her breasts, down across her tight stomach to the well of her navel.

"You *are* beautiful," he said. "You're the most beautiful woman I've ever seen."

Ariel opened her mouth to protest, then shut it again when the look in Jacob's eyes told her that was serious. He meant it.

He let his fingers slide around her waist, then ran them up to her breasts again, the movement so light that Ariel shivered. Her body broke out in delicious gooseflesh. He moved his fingers back down to her rounded hips and then allowed them to drift even lower, watching Ariel's face as her eyes began to glow with desire, her lips parting slightly with anticipation. Reaching the tuft that hid Ariel's sex he ran his fingers through it, feeling the drops of moisture that clung there. He moved his fingers into the soft, slick folds of her labia.

Both of them began to breathe more quickly as Jacob's fingers moved against the most sensitive parts of Ariel's body. Spreading her folds with his other hand, Jacob dipped two fingers inside her, his thumb on her clit. Pressing, circling with his fingers, he caressed Ariel until she writhed and gasped.

Unable to resist tasting her, he lowered his head between her legs and groaned at the sweetness collected there. Two fingers still inside her, he laved her soft bud with his practiced tongue. Ariel let out gorgeous moans of pure abandon. Jacob felt his penis swell to the point of bursting. He seized her full buttocks and kept her trapped against his mouth as she tried to buck him away.

"Oh, oh, yes, please, oh," she was crying incoherently, frenzied by her need. As she came, she arched herself into him, her hands in his hair, rocking her hips with the rhythm of her climax. He released her and held himself above her, gazing into her flushed, nearly delirious face.

Jacob didn't think she could imagine how hard she made him.

Feeling her swollen vulva press against his lips, tasting the welling moisture that his touch brought forth, clasping her hips with his arms while the waves of her orgasm rolled through her had almost been enough to make him come, too . . .

Almost.

As her body stilled and her muscles loosened, he quickly stripped off what remained of his clothing. Working his way up her body now, he kissed each part of it he'd run his finger down before. Then claimed her mouth. She gave herself up to his kiss completely.

Jacob's penis was rock-hard against the inside of Ariel's silky thigh. Asking with his eyes, he received his answer immediately. She was ready for him again.

Holding himself with one hand, he parted her lower lips with the other. She opened to receive all of him. Each time she shifted her hips, Jacob felt that she'd accepted him more fully, somehow taken him deeper into her center. Everything was electricity, fire. He moved into her again and again, groaning with exultation. This was better than any sex he'd ever experienced—better, maybe, than being on the pedestal at the Paris-Roubaix.

He'd never thought he'd be able to say that about anything.

Pushing the length of his throbbing penis again and again into Ariel's heated depths, cradling her face as he kissed her full lips, kneading her breasts and clutching her waist and hips to bring her more tightly against him, to lock their bodies together in a melting embrace, he wondered if he'd ever feel anything this good again. He remembered Ariel's words: *We have all night for the longer stages . . .*

What stage were they on? It was impossible to tell. With Ariel, it seemed like the race never ended, like there would always be new heights to scale, new peaks, new triumphs . . .

He knew he would never get tired of the ride.

Then sensation overwhelmed him, erasing everything but the feeling of Ariel's body against him, around him, and he exploded inside her.

*

When Ariel came back to her senses, she realized she was clinging to Jacob. Her fingertips dug into the muscles of his back. Her thighs squeezed his lean hips. He pushed himself up on his arms, and she thought for a moment he was trying to pull away from her.

But he wasn't. He had just lifted himself off her so that he could gaze down at her. The look in his eyes melted her completely. Even though she'd seen him look at her like that before, she could never quite believe it.

He loved her.

He hadn't said it yet, but those golden eyes couldn't lie. Ariel stretched her arms above her head and arched up. He lowered his head to kiss her breasts. He kissed her throat. Bit playfully at her lips.

Jacob Hunter loved her. The knowledge blossomed inside of her. It felt nourishing. Exciting. Did he know it? Had he admitted it to himself?

Ariel felt a moment of panic. It wouldn't last. She wouldn't be able to hold Jacob Hunter's attention. She would have fallen permanently, irrevocably in love with him, and he would be gone, speeding through the Pyrenees toward his next romantic liaison.

I need to leave this bed, she thought. *I need to protect myself. I need to run away before it's too late.*

There were many reasons why a relationship with Jacob Hunter wouldn't work. He was a gorgeous, famous cyclist with an international female fan club. She was a career girl who had enough trouble making time to date men from other boroughs, let alone men guided from country to country . . . well, by the pole star.

To top it all off, she had lied to him about who she was. She had been sent to Colorado to essentially ruin his reputation. Maybe the muckrakers were right. Maybe Jacob Hunter used drugs.

She didn't think so. She wanted to defend him.

Even if it cost her a job.

Her mind started racing and Jacob could see the cloud cross her emerald eyes. "What are you thinking?" he asked her.

"I should go back to my room," she said. "I should . . . I mean . . . it's late . . . You need your rest, your strength . . . "

"I need you, Ariel," said Jacob. He kissed her and she moaned, half-desire, half-desperation.

This affair with Jacob Hunter was going to be a mess. She could think of a million reasons why she should get up and leave. But her body and her heart had another agenda.

Don't think any more tonight.

She linked her arms around Jacob's neck. "Sorry," she said. "I forgot about your legendary endurance. And you forgot something about me."

"Hmmmm." Jacob grinned. "What would that be?"

"My legendary dancer's flexibility," Ariel whispered.

Jacob's eyes widened. "Your legendary dancer's flexibility," he repeated, a wicked smile lighting up his handsome face. "What exactly do you mean by that?"

So Ariel showed him. Until the morning sun came through the window.

Chapter Ten

Ariel woke up late . . . in Jacob's hotel room. But Jacob was gone. She didn't remember when he'd left her. She'd been deeply asleep. He'd leaned over her and whispered that he was going to train, that she should stay as long as she liked. She remained in his room almost until noon. She showered, humming, enjoying the spray of the hot water against her skin and the smell of the lavender-scented shower gel. The Alpenhof, she thought with approval, got everything right—even the water pressure. But then, as she stepped out of the shower, she was struck by an unwelcome memory.

Today was the day she'd arranged to meet Brian Jenks.

Ariel sat on the side of Jacob's bed for a long time. She tried to sort out her tangled emotions as she towel-dried her long hair.

More than anything, she felt guilty. Any attempt on her part to prove the allegations of Jacob's drug use true would be a betrayal of her feelings for him, and of his for her. Could she trust him entirely? Her instincts told her that he was on the up-and-up. But should she take that for granted? Especially if she was considering becoming deeply personally involved with him? Or if . . . she took a breath . . . or if she already *was* deeply involved with him?

Personally. Physically. Emotionally. Utterly. Involved.

She still felt deeply curious about what had happened between Jacob and Jenks. Now that she knew him better, she couldn't imagine Jacob being involved in a bar room brawl unless there were something important at stake. Sure, he could be touchy, prickly—she'd borne the brunt of it, until he'd warmed to her—but she couldn't believe he was needlessly violent. She'd seen him behave with such compassion, such gentleness.

Her personal and journalistic curiosity was goading her to

keep the meeting with Jenks. Whatever she found out would help her to understand Jacob better. *I don't have to use the information against him,* she thought. It sounded a lot like an attempt at self-justification, even to her.

Once she'd made her decision, Ariel turned her thoughts to the distance between Jacob's room and her own. She considered her two options. Option one: the walk of shame. She could slink back to her room in the same dress she'd worn last night, hopelessly rumpled. Or she could go the short distance down the hall and down the elevator in a robe. Guests did it all the time, coming to or from the pool.

Leaving her dress and pumps in Jacob's room, she walked outside barefoot, in the terry robe from Jacob's bathroom. Jacob had left one of his key cards on the bedside table, and she slipped it in the pocket of the robe on the way out so she could come back and retrieve her things later.

Back in her room, she felt jazzed, energetic. After a few moments shifting through her notepads, she threw down her pen and changed into workout clothes. Thirty minutes on the treadmill followed by an hour at machines later, she felt good. Strong. Her hard workout had barely sapped her strength. She was hungry, yes. But tired . . . not at all.

Ariel strode purposefully through Vail Village. She knew exactly what she wanted. An avocado shake. Why not? She was pretty sure it was going to taste a lot better than her usual midday snack of trail mix and apples.

She looked around the café as she ordered her shake, half-hoping she would run into Steven and Randall. Maybe they'd whisk her away to wherever Jacob had gone to train and she could spend the afternoon in the sun, drinking her avocado shake and watching Jacob's body make spandex into a downright *sin.*

That sounded a whole lot better to her than meeting up with Brian Jenks.

She left the café and sat on the hood of her car finishing her shake. It was weird, but delicious. Not the kind of thing she'd drink in New York. But then again, Ariel had been doing all kinds of things she didn't do in New York. A few elderly women passed by on the sidewalk and smiled at her. Ariel smiled back. Then she sighed and stood up. No one was going to save her from her decision. She had an appointment to keep.

As Ariel drove, she had to admit to herself she liked the sporty rental coupe. She liked the way it jumped forward however lightly she pressed the accelerator, the way it cornered, totally responsive to her steering. Jacob wasn't the only one who loved speed.

She smiled as her thoughts returned to him—his warmth, his intense, golden eyes fixed on hers, his beautiful body, his commitment to his sport, the passion his touch aroused. She wondered again what she was doing, trying to dig up dirt up on his personal life. Journalists made everything their business. But she was more than a journalist now, to Jacob. She owed him more.

She headed out of Vail. Some of the mountain slopes were timbered; others were bare—brown and yellow with arid grasses, gray and red with glittering rocks, dotted with white and gold wildflowers. She couldn't deny the beauty of the terrain, but as she wound her way through the canyons, she felt that there was something forbidding about it, too. The landscape looked hard. Above, the cloudless sky was a blinding plain.

In rural New York, the hills were low and rolling. She'd raked enough rocks from her father's garden plot to know that the soil wasn't exactly *soft*, but it was rich and dark and wet, thick with worms. The sky was tiny, a mellow blue, veiled with mists or pillowy with drifting white clouds. Without Jacob by her side, she felt out of place in this alien terrain.

What was it like in the winter? She didn't want to imagine the driving snow, the wind and ice. Even in summer, she could sense the latent power of the Rockies. They held entire glaciers in their crags. They could make their own weather. These mountains were so much younger than the weathered New England hills. They were still volatile. Violent.

Ariel was in a strange, flighty mood. When she pulled into Minturn, it was easy to find The Minturn Saloon, where she'd agreed to meet Jenks for a late lunch. Minturn, like Vail, had been developed by its tourist industry, but it retained more of the feel of a frontier town. Looking at the old brick saloon, she felt suddenly like she was in the Old West. This was railroad country. Mining country. She could hear the sound of rushing water. The Eagle River?

She stared at her hands still clutching the steering wheel. Conflicting impulses warred within her. The first: to learn Jacob's secret. The second: to respect his privacy. To trust him.

She couldn't make herself get out of the car.

What could Brian Jenks possibly tell her that she should believe more than what she'd felt in Jacob's touch, seen in his eyes: that he was an honorable man, someone she could believe in. Despite his strange behavior, she trusted him.

She loved him.

She started the car. Jacob had stood her up for lunch on her first day in Colorado. Now she was standing up Brian Jenks. It was some kind of weird domino effect. Maybe just the presence of a New Yorker in Colorado was making the place less friendly. Oh well.

She decided to drive through Minturn—what little there was of it. These tiny houses . . . were they vacation rentals? Or were these the economic homes of people who lived and worked here year round? While researching, she had glanced at the demographics of different towns in Eagle County but she couldn't remember the population. She wondered if there was an opera house. Didn't all Old West towns have opera houses? She drove slowly down the short side streets and turned back onto Main Street.

Ariel continued to drive slowly, no longer looking around, lost in thought. It was only when she passed The Minturn Saloon that something caught her eye. A Ducati Monster roaring out onto the road in front of her. It was Jacob.

What was he doing? He'd said he was going to training. But it didn't seem like he'd be training at The Mintrurn Saloon. And he certainly wasn't carrying a bicycle with him.

Ariel's pulse thundered in her ears. She'd quelled her curiosity once today. She'd thrown away her chance at speaking with Brian Jenks. She couldn't resist her curiosity now. She jerked the wheel sharply, pulling in front of the Saloon for the second time that day. She waited, engine idling, until a truck passed. Then she pulled out again. She could see Jacob pulling away down the road, a few car-lengths ahead of the truck. Luckily the truck too was putting on speed. The distance closed.

She shook her head at herself. *A tiger can't change its stripes,* she thought. *I can't stop being a journalist just because I'm in love.* Tailing Jacob to his destination didn't seem hopelessly immoral. It was better than meeting with a man who hated him, who'd fought with him and who would doubtlessly spin Jacob's behavior in the worst possible light.

This would give her her sleuthing fix and hopefully provide her with a crumb to feed to Theo—who she could only imagine was losing all hope for her.

Why had Jacob lied to her, anyway? She was certain he had *something* to hide. At this point, she didn't think it was drug use. She couldn't imagine Jacob cheating . . . after seeing the passion he had for the sport, hearing him talk about his love for racing. He had the kind of commitment that couldn't be faked and couldn't be compromised. She believed he was clean. Not that that explained certain other strange aspects of his behavior. Like his evasiveness with journalists. Like lying to her about where he was going.

She was frustrated when a semi pulled in front of her and

blocked Jacob from view. By the time the truck turned away to the right, he was no longer in sight. She had lost him. She'd have no juicy tidbit to offer Theo.

On her drive back to the hotel, she tried to imagine what she would, in fact, say to Theo. She'd have to call him when she got back to the hotel to apprise him of her progress . . . or lack thereof. She couldn't give him the story he wanted. The only story she could imagine writing about Jacob would be a profile of a man who was beautiful in more ways than one. Whose athleticism and self-discipline were unparalleled, and whose successes were honestly won.

She wondered how she'd be able to work in a salacious passage on his hot bod. She knew she wouldn't be able to resist offering her readers an opportunity to vicariously appreciate *all* the things she loved about Jacob. And sex sold magazines, right?

She wasn't sure if Theo would go for it. And if he didn't, she couldn't see any way to avoid having the story canned . . . and going back to New York. When she thought about leaving Colorado, she experienced a deep ache—somewhere in the vicinity of her heart.

*

Ariel decided to stop off at Jacob's room to pick up her clothes before she dealt with Theo. Letting herself in with Jacob's key, she saw that the suite had been cleaned and looked as dazzlingly luxurious as it had the first time she saw it. The bed had been freshly made, her discarded dress folded and laid on a chair. She felt a moment of embarrassment as she imagined what the maids must have thought when they encountered the rumpled bed and the discarded woman's clothing. The room must have looked like the scene of a debauch.

Collecting her things, she wondered when she'd see Jacob again. They hadn't made any plans to meet later. Smiling, she realized she'd grown very quickly to expect that they'd see one another every day . . . and definitely, *definitely* every night. She moved to the desk in the sitting room to find paper for a note. She'd leave him something teasing, suggestive. Something that would make him look forward to their next meeting as much as she did.

But what she saw when she slid open the desk drawer shocked her so much she dropped her dress and her shoes to the floor. With a trembling hand, she picked up the small baggy of white powder she'd found within.

Her heart pounding, she slipped it into her pocket.

Then she snatched up her clothes and stumbled blindly from the room.

Chapter Eleven

Jacob was buzzed through the gate and walked along the flower-bordered path. The grounds were small but cheerful, with garden beds bright with purple kale and cherry tomatoes, and a picnic table in a cluster of young aspens.

Two young women were sitting at the picnic table. They looked equally happy, equally at ease in the warm afternoon, although Jacob knew that one of them had to be a patient, the other a nurse. This was a wonderful facility. It didn't look like a hospital. The main building was a beautiful, three-story house with a communal kitchen, a library, an entertainment room, and private bedrooms for all the residents. The mental health nurses, therapists, and drug counselors were some of the best in the state. All in all, it was a wonderful place for a troubled girl to make a full recovery.

Jacob was glad he could afford it. His parents hadn't wanted to ask him for money. He'd only been pro for a few years. The money had just begun to roll in, and he'd already used a big chunk of it to pay his father's medical debt and the mortgage on the house. But when Jacob had flown home and seen his sister, ninety-five pounds, rocking in the corner of her bedroom, he'd squelched all protests with a single grim stare.

"Whatever it takes," he'd said, voice breaking as he knelt by his sister and put his arms around her. He looked back at his parents, the two of them framed in the doorway. "Karen, Mom, Dad," he'd said. "We're all in this together. Karen, we're going to do whatever it takes to get you through this."

Even now, though, it was hard to believe that the situation had gotten so bad so fast. Jacob's father never talked about it. What he thought was anyone's guess. But Jacob knew he had to feel bad.

Had to feel in some ways responsible. Jacob knew his mother felt a lot of guilt. He sure as hell did. Karen had gone right to the edge, and no one had stopped her. Why hadn't anyone known sooner? Intervened sooner? She could be in jail right now. Or worse. His beautiful, brilliant, caring little sister could be dead.

Another addict. Another statistic. Jacob felt the hot tears rise in his eyes. He had to stop for a moment in the path and collect himself.

"Hi," said one of the women at the picnic table. "Those are pretty." Jacob smiled. He carried a bag of goodies—apples, oranges, granola bars, a few of squares of dark chocolate—and a cluster of columbines he'd picked on the side of the road. He waved at them with the columbines.

"Have a tomato," said the other woman. She sounded proud. Jacob knew that gardening was incorporated into the therapy here. Planting seeds, tending the soil—these activities connected people to the earth, to the rhythms of life. Helping something grow *should* make you feel empowered.

"Love to," he said, approaching the garden and plucking a ripe cherry tomato form the vine. It was prickly in his mouth, then warm and sweet. He took a moment to collect himself, looking at the lovingly weeded rows of leafy greens and the short trellises of peas.

It was terrifying how close they'd come to losing Karen. It was more terrifying to think she wasn't out of the woods yet. At least here, she had professional support. She could garden. She could sit at a picnic table and read a book while the aspens quaked in the breeze. Sure, it wasn't quite like living a normal life. There were single and group meetings every day, planned activities, people constantly looking over her shoulder. Her horizons were limited by the gates, the walls. But she was safe. She had time and space enough to dream of something beyond this limited world: a bigger, better tomorrow. He wanted that for her. A bright future, full of love and hope. He'd do anything to help her get it.

Five years younger than he was, Jacob's sister Karen had always been a sunny, vivacious girl, dominating dinner table discussions with boisterous tales of her playground exploits. Jacob had taught her how to ride a bike, had spent entire winters pulling her up the sledding hill in the old toboggan so she could shoot down again, screaming bloody murder.

But by the time she was in high school, Jacob was out of the house, traveling around the country racing. He was surprised when he saw her at Christmas the first year he'd spent away from home. He knew kids changed a lot during adolescence, but the alteration in his kid sister had seemed dramatic. She didn't seem to have her former sparkle, but that could have been due to her teenage angst, which Jacob could only assume prompted her decision to dye her blond hair shiny black.

"You look like you're in the Addams family," he'd joked and for the first time his ribbing had fallen flat with his sister, who fixed him with a contemptuous sneer.

"A phase," his mother whispered in the kitchen as Jacob helped her make the gravy for the Christmas goose. "It's just a phase. Like when you wouldn't let anyone cut off that God-awful rat-tail."

"I looked good with that rat-tail," protested Jacob and he and his mother collapsed into the warming laughter that had always sustained their relationship. Still, Jacob could tell his mother was worried. Karen was sensitive and had been deeply affected by their father's blindness and subsequent depression. It didn't make it easier that money was tight and she was a teenage girl facing all the usual social pressures: pressures to have the right clothes, the right car, the right zip code.

Colorado was a state of geographical and social extremes. It attracted a rich crowd, tourists who flew to the Rockies for ski vacations, but not enough of the tourism revenue trickled down to the struggling families. Jacob knew from experience that it was hard to grow up in close proximity to people who had so much when you had very little yourself. Well, little in some respects. Even when Jacob's father was able to work, the family had had to scrimp on luxuries. But they never scrimped on love. That was the important thing.

However, Jacob had to recognize the fact that after his father's eyes got too bad for him to drive, the atmosphere in the home had become strained. Always a robust man, not talkative, no, but active, with a lively, penetrating gaze, Richard Hunter now took to sitting in the living room armchair with the lights off. He wore dark glasses and it was hard to tell if he was asleep or awake. He didn't seem to want company, and he never showed any interest in his daughter. Karen, who used to chatter at his side for hours after the evening news, would now cross the room along the back wall or else avoid the living room all together. She would come downstairs and walk out the front door, entering the kitchen through the side door. Not a good situation.

Two years ago, Karen had dropped out of school before earning her teaching certificate—and Jacob hadn't found out for months. His mother took a while to tell him the news, and Karen herself had become increasingly hard to reach by phone. Jacob finally learned that she'd left Denver, had come back to Leadville. She hadn't moved back home, though. Instead, she'd moved in with her boyfriend.

By then, Jacob was racing in Europe and spending even more time away from Colorado. Jacob called Karen using the Internet phone almost every night when he was training in Italy and left messages but she didn't return his calls or emails. It was odd timing . . . just as his career was taking off, family tensions were starting to weigh him down. He tried to shrug it off, focus on where he was, what he was doing. But the Hunters were a close-knit bunch and the past years of not-quite-right were taking their toll on him. He couldn't shake the suspicion that not quite right was about to get a whole lot wrong. It helped that he was starting to earn enough to send his family money, but it still didn't feel like enough.

Jacob could hear the weariness in his mother's voice when they talked on the phone. Nonetheless, she was always filled with funny anecdotes about her work as a school nurse ("Not just a penny, Jacob! This little boy had a roll of quarters up his nose!" "Inflation, Mom.") and she never failed to tell him how proud she was of his cycling. He sent DVDs of his races home, but he was afraid to ask if Dad watched them. Richard could see the television screen if he sat very close, but he rarely he did so. Too much effort. Everything about him indicated utter resignation. He'd given up.

This from the man who had taught Jacob how to fly.

When Jacob got the call—the call he'd been half-expecting— he was in France.

"Come back, Jakey," his mother had said. "Karen needs you."

He got on the first flight home.

His mother had warned him. He'd thought he was prepared to see Karen. He wasn't. His sister had lost thirty pounds. She'd shown up at their parents' house in the middle of the night to ask for money.

They had to face the hard truth: Karen was addicted to meth.

Jacob entered the rehab center and greeted the house manager.

"Hi, Jake," said Bettina, a kind, maternal woman with large, dark eyes. "Let's check the bag." She went through the snacks in Jacob's bag quickly and perfunctorily, making sure he hadn't brought his sister cigarettes or other controlled substances.

"Looks good," she said. "Healthy."

He walked past the library, saw people reading, a few others sitting at laptops. No Karen. He peeked in the kitchen. It looked a tornado had hit. There were bags of flour and sugar, mixing bowls, and pots on every surface. Jacob caught a snatch of a heated argument about leavening reduction at high altitude. He grinned. Nothing quite like baking a birthday cake at ten thousand feet. He recognized some of the residents, and some of the nurses and attendants from previous visits, and he gave a little nod before moving on. He was certain they recognized him, even if they hadn't seen him here before. Everyone recognized him these days.

But no one reacted as though a celebrity had just burst onto the scene.

Discretion. That was key. Having Karen's battle with addiction become a matter of public interest due to his sudden fame would be the worst thing Jacob could imagine.

Karen planned to teach kindergarten. A reputation as a recovering meth-head would hurt her chances, maybe permanently. Certainly in Colorado. Karen would have to leave the state.

Maybe it would be good for her to get away. But it had to be her own decision. Jacob wouldn't let her be forced out of town by shame and notoriety. Not if he could help it. Even if he had to lie to reporters about his family. Even if he had to make up stories to explain where he went when he disappeared on his motorcycle. When Jacob had first read articles that attributed his stellar racing record and attention-dodging behavior to performance drug abuse, he'd almost laughed. He actually preferred the rumors to the questions . . . questions that might lead the press closer to the real drama in the Hunter family. After all, the accusations were ultimately harmless. Jacob's tests were squeaky clean. He'd never dreamed of using drugs to help his race. It was antithetical to who he was, what he stood for.

On one hand, racing in the Colorado Classic was a dream come true. On the other, racing in Colorado brought all the scrutiny he feared too close to home.

His fight with Brian had been a disaster. It was covered in multiple local papers and it was a miracle that, as far as he knew, no large national or international paper had picked up the story. Yet. No one knew how Brian Jenks was connected to Jacob Hunter. His sister's boyfriend. His sister's dealer.

Ex-boyfriend, Jacob reminded himself. *Ex*-dealer.

Jacob crossed the hall and knocked lightly on Karen's door. After a moment, the door cracked open and Jacob was looking into his sister's large, hazel eyes.

"Jakey," she said, and threw the door open. She was wearing loose cargo pants and a long sleeve shirt that cloaked her painfully thin frame. Jacob followed her into her room and placed the bag of snacks on the table. Karen took the columbines from his hand and touched their petals lovingly.

"My favorite," she said solemnly.

Jacob smiled. "I brought you dark chocolate, too," he said.

"My *real* favorite," crowed Karen, tearing into the bag with impish delight.

Jacob was happy seeing his sister displaying her former vivacity. She'd decorated the walls of the small, antiseptic room with a kitten calendar, pictures of Jacob that she'd cut from cycling magazines and a few older family photos. The top of her dresser was covered with books and notebooks. It looked like her dresser back home.

Karen launched into stories about the staff, the other patients in her group, her drug counselor, and her plans to reenter college in the fall semester. Jacob noticed that her face was pale and that her words tumbled out faster and faster. She was sweating and when he went to put a hand on her shoulder, to get her to slow down, she jerked away from him.

Jacob's heart sank.

"Have you had any other visitors today, Karen?" he asked levelly. Karen didn't meet his eyes. She threw herself on her narrow bed.

"I can ask the nurses if you won't tell me," he said.

Karen sat up. "Why shouldn't Brian come to see me?" she asked in a high, shrill voice. "He *loves* me. We've been through a lot together."

"He's put you through a lot," said Jacob. He sat next to Karen on the bed and she flinched away from him. Jacob's fury mounted as he thought about what kinds of experiences had made Karen so skittish. "Karen," he said. "You've always been our family's source of strength. Your energy has always held us together."

"It hasn't been enough," said Karen, her face twisted in pain. Jacob heard the eerie echo of his own fears. *I couldn't do enough.* Couldn't make his father see again. Couldn't erase his sister's suffering.

"But *you* are enough," said Jacob. "Just you. Being who you are. You need to take care of yourself. You need to channel your strength and energy into loving yourself. Karen, we don't need anything from you but for you to be healthy and happy."

"Brian loves me," said Karen again. Her shoulders shook. "Jakey . . . I feel so lost."

Jacob reached out slowly and stroked his sister's hair. "Did he bring you drugs, Karen?"

Karen nodded, stifling sobs with her fist. She pointed at the dresser and Jacob rifled through the top drawer until he found the tiny bag. It wasn't the first time. Jacob had found drugs in Karen's room before. He hadn't told his parents or the staff because he hadn't wanted to jeopardize Karen's placement in the treatment center. Stupidly, he'd thought he could handle the situation himself. But apparently knocking Brian Jenks's lights out hadn't done the trick.

Earlier in the day he'd driven to Minturn looking for Brian, hoping to have another go at it. Not at putting the man's lights out, necessarily, but at coming to an understanding. He'd gone to a house where he'd heard Brian had been doing some odd-job carpentry, and then to The Minturn Saloon. He'd gone prepared to buy him off. To give him the money to go to another state, to build a meth lab in California, to start a meth empire for all Jacob cared. He just wanted the man as far from his sister as possible.

But he hadn't found Brian, and now he was glad. He knew the idea of giving Brian Jenks money was utterly irresponsible. Maybe even evil. Brian Jenks would buy filthy drugs and sell them to *somebody's* sister. He couldn't let that happen. But what could he do? He couldn't keep beating him up. Jacob was at a loss.

After the fight that night, he'd gone back to the hotel in a daze, dreading the inevitable fall-out. If the fight was widely publicized, it could reveal Jacob's secret after all—and ruin Karen's life. He'd avoided the hotel staff and his teammates as best he could that night, and in the few days to follow. He'd had bruises and cuts on his face, but it was some consolation to know that Brian looked worse.

Jacob had been remarkably unfocused on his training. Absentminded. Forgetful. No one knew that his mind was spinning, racing to find a solution to the terrible reality of Karen's addiction and the danger of Jenks's influence without jeopardizing the whole family's pressing need for secrecy.

He couldn't even remember what he'd done with the drugs he'd confiscated from Karen the last time. A cold chill swept through him. They must still be in his room somewhere. What if someone found them? One of the maids? If they went to the press, hoping to benefit from his notoriety, his whole carefully built house of cards could topple down around his ears. He would look for them and throw them away along with this day's batch as soon as he got back.

He looked at the little bag in his palm. He looked at it so hard it was like he was trying to shoot a laser beam with his eyes and zap the bag out of existence. *Damn Brian Jenks to hell.*

Now that this had happened a second time it was clear to him that he couldn't deal with the situation alone. He needed backup. From the staff. From his parents. Maybe from the police— although he would only go to them as a last resort.

"I've got to report this," Jacob said. "Karen, I'm sorry. He can't see you. He's poison for you."

"Jakey, no," Karen said, eyes wild. "If you talk to the staff they'll kick me out. I can't go home yet. I'm not ready. I need more time. I need more help. Jakey, please. I know that you're right about Brian. I know he's bad for me. But I'm all he's got."

"Maybe," said Jacob. "But he's not all you've got, Karen. You have a family. You have a future. You're a giver, Karen. Many men will love and need you throughout your life. You have to be careful. You have to keep your heart safe and only give it to the man who will help you protect it. Cherish it."

"What if I don't find him?" whispered Karen.

"You will," said Jacob. He thought of Ariel, her sensitivity, her warmth, the way she looked into his eyes and seemed to understand everything about him. If he could find someone he could trust with his heart, Karen could, too. He was sure of it. He realized that he wanted Ariel to meet Karen. He didn't want to keep his life compartmentalized anymore. He was tired of secrets.

"I won't talk to the staff about the drugs," said Jacob. "But we're going to tell them that Brian Jenks isn't allowed to visit anymore. We're going to tell them right now. Together."

"Okay," said Karen.

"And next time I come," said Jacob. "I'm going to bring someone special to introduce to you. I think you'll like her."

Karen gave a wobbly smile. "I bet I will, Jakey. If she's willing to put up with you, I think she's crazy enough to fit in with us Hunters."

"I hope so," Jacob said. "I hope so."

Jacob looked forward to seeing Ariel again the whole way back into town. He went over the events of the previous night in his mind, turning each moment over like a precious treasure. Ariel had given herself to him unreservedly. He was ready to do the same for her—to make a gift of himself, his heart, the truth about his family and his life. She was a reporter. But somehow he knew that their connection meant more to her now than her assignment, her professional responsibilities. He trusted her.

Besides, she was only writing a celebrity profile. From what he'd seen of those in the past, she wouldn't have to dig too deep to give the magazine's readership a satisfyingly superficial account of Jacob Hunter, the cycling star. He'd tell her some anecdotes about cycling in Europe, his camaraderie with his teammates, whatever she needed to paint a shallow picture of Jacob as an athlete—and a man—with nothing to hide.

When he got back to his room, he suffered a minor feeling of disappointment to see that Ariel wasn't there any longer. It would be ridiculous if she were. Had he really imagined she'd lie in bed all day waiting for him? Of course not. But he liked the idea of it . . . of seeing her still stretched out in his bed, warm and naked, sleeping late after their night of wild abandon, which had lasted until the early hours of the morning.

He called her cell, and was surprised when she didn't answer. He'd gotten used to the assumption that he was her priority during her time in Colorado. Her interview subject. And, finally, her lover. *Maybe I need an ego check*, he thought ruefully.

Maybe she was in the shower? He checked her room, but there was no answer to his knock, and he didn't hear anything from within.

Frustrated, he wandered back to his room, feeling aimless now that he couldn't find her, couldn't make a clean breast of it as he'd planned, couldn't invite her to meet his sister. His parents. He was surprised to realize how much he wanted her around— *permanently*. This wasn't a one-week kind of feeling. It wasn't a one-month feeling, or even one year.

It was a one-lifetime feeling. A once in one-lifetime kind of love.

He had to do something to work off some of his physical and mental energy. The day had already been a rollercoaster ride. It left him feeling keyed up, jittery. His rest days were sometimes harder than his days of hard training. He was accustomed to so much physical activity. When he didn't get it, he felt oddly off-balance. And there were so many hours in the day when you didn't spend five of them on a bicycle.

Usually he spent his time off the bike loading up on high calorie foods, hanging out with his teammates or with Liz, and reading voraciously. People who got close to him were always surprised to learn that Jacob Hunter was a bookworm. It had always been his second favorite activity, his second favorite escape from mundane reality. In the past few years he'd had hardly any time to indulge in his literary habit, but he crammed a little in here and there—a few pages at a time in a hotel room, a team RV, or an airport.

Today he knew he wouldn't be able to concentrate on *One Hundred Years of Solitude*. Wouldn't be able to keep all the characters, their names repeating from generation to generation, straight in his head. It required serious mental effort at the best of times. Today there was no chance. He grabbed his towel and changed into swim trunks. *When in doubt,* he thought, *go swimming.*

When he exited the elevator on the hotel's roof he saw that another hotel guest had had the same idea. With a rush of pleasure—and desire—he realized it was Ariel's incomparable form slipping gracefully through the cool water. He dived in behind her and swam quickly to catch up. *Just like the first time,* he thought.

*

They came up for air within feet of each other. As soon as Ariel saw Jacob—his warm smile, his gorgeous eyes catching the light of the afternoon sun—her heart did a weird flip in her chest. She'd come to the pool to collect herself, to soothe her jangling nerves, to plan what she'd do next. She hadn't known what she'd say when she saw Jacob again—and she still didn't.

She wanted to swim to him, to kiss him, to taste his lips again as she had last night. And simultaneously she felt that a wall had grown up between them. A wall that made kissing Jacob ever again seem impossible.

She'd been crying. She was glad that the wetness of the pool water on her cheeks hid it from him.

*

Jacob knew something was wrong—very wrong. Ariel's face was beautiful, as always. But she was looking as him as if he'd killed her kitten. As if he'd betrayed her horribly in some way. As if her heart was breaking.

To his shock, she turned her back on him and swam to the side of the pool, pulling herself out as if she couldn't stand to share the water with him. She was halfway to the elevator before he caught up with her.

"Ariel!" he yelled, and she paused without turning around. He passed her and wheeled around to face her, blocking her path. He stepped closer and rested his hands lightly on her shoulders. She dropped her head, refusing to meet his eyes. A tear rolled down her cheek and he saw it, caught it with his finger, gently wiping it away. He looked at her, questioning, but she wasn't looking at him. He had to ask.

"What is it? What's happened?" He tilted up her chin. "Look at me."

He gazed into the welling emerald depths of her eyes. He let his hands drop to her shoulders, tried to envelop her in a hug.

"Don't touch me," she said softly, and then bit her lower lip in a way that reminded him of his little sister, that sent a surge of love and sadness sweeping through him, a desire to protect her against whatever it was that was hurting her—except that, given the way she was acting, it seemed as if he himself were the source of her pain.

He let her go, watching her walk to the elevator, not sure if he should follow her or not.

His indecision only lasted a moment—just long enough for the elevator doors to close, hiding Ariel from his view. He waited impatiently for it to come up again, toweling himself dry as he did so.

He exited at Ariel's floor and jogged down the hallway to the door of her room. Knocking, he hoped like hell she'd answer.

*

Ariel looked up from where she sat on the side of her hotel bed when she heard Jacob's knock. She stared at the door blankly. She wasn't ready for this. But she'd have to face him eventually. Might as well get it over with. She opened the door and backed away from it, her arms crossed over her chest, as Jacob entered warily.

"Ariel?" he asked. She jolted as her body responded uncontrollably, unconsciously, to his nearness, the husky richness of his voice. "Talk to me. Please. Tell me what's wrong."

It was torture to hear the pleading tone in his voice, the genuine uncertainty. To see his brow furrowed with concern. Had he truly imagined she wouldn't find out?

"Jacob," she said, trying to keep her voice neutral, "I found this in your desk drawer. I was looking for paper to write you a note."

Jacob stared blankly at the tiny plastic bag Ariel held out on her palm. "It's not mine," he said levelly, raising his eyes to meet hers.

Ariel's voice broke as she cried, "Don't lie to me, Jacob. Everyone says you're using drugs to win races. I was beginning to think they were wrong. How could I have been so naïve?"

Jacob shook his head, half annoyed, half confused. "You've got one thing wrong for sure, Ariel," he said. "Performance enhancing drugs don't look anything like that. What you've got there is methamphetamine."

Ariel's eyes widened. She dropped the baggie on the ground as if it were a poisonous snake. "That's supposed to be *better?*" she hissed furiously.

Jacob closed the distance between them and wrapped his arms around her.

Ariel was stiff as a board in his arms. Then she dropped her head against his chest, raised her hands to either side of his waist. She couldn't feel furious, betrayed, when he held her like this. Simply couldn't. No matter what he'd done. Jacob pulled her against him and she was plunged back into the overwhelming array of sensations she'd felt the night before. The air around them seemed to crackle with electricity. Ariel's mind was saying one thing, her body—all her senses—saying something else. Saying, against all the evidence and all the strength of her rational thinking, *You can trust this man.*

As if he'd read her mind, Jacob brushed his lips against her ear, whispering, "Trust me." She let herself relax completely against him, pressing the length of her body into his. She was responding to him instinctively, from the feeling in her gut. Not the way she was accustomed to operating.

Jacob's arm tightened around Ariel's waist, lifting her onto her toes. He sank his other hand into the voluminous mass of her hair and kissed her passionately, completely shattering her last defenses.

"There's an explanation," he murmured but she stopped his lips with her finger.

"Not now," she said. "If I trust you . . . " Her words came slowly, as though she were figuring out how she felt even as she spoke. "If I trust you . . . I don't need an explanation. I don't need proof. Trust isn't about evidence. It's something else. Something riskier and deeper. It's like . . . "

She'd almost said love.

"Faith," he finished. His grip was so tight it hurt.

"I will prove to you that your trust wasn't misplaced, Ariel Hayes," he whispered.

"I know," she said. "Later."

Chapter Twelve

Ariel came to consciousness slowly. It was the middle of the night. The room was dark. Her body felt warm . . . good. Too warm . . . too good . . .

Memory flooded back and she returned to her senses. Her senses told her that she was in bed with Jacob Hunter. Her legs were entwined with his. One of his arms was thrown over her hip. Every part of her welcomed his weight. His warmth. She felt fantastic.

It was a mistake, of course. Jumping into bed with Jacob after finding meth in his hotel room was obviously a mistake.

But it had to be the best mistake she'd ever made.

Ariel ran her fingertips over Jacob's shoulder. As always, his sharply defined muscles made her catch her breath. Maybe she was the one with the problem. Maybe she was the one who was out of control.

She was addicted to Jacob Hunter.

She couldn't say no to that body . . . to those gorgeous golden eyes . . . that demanding mouth. She couldn't suppress her cravings. She wanted him all the time. Her better judgment was powerless against her baser urges. He was so damn irresistible. It wasn't just his perfect butt, or his masculine jaw line, or the way he looked at her, the way his expression could change from sleepy-sexy to super-intense in less than a split second. It was his confidence, his wit, his flashes of surprising sweetness and sensitivity . . . .

For god's sake, the man could even quote from her father's favorite Shakespeare play. He had used his knowledge of *The Tempest* and what she'd told him about her kind, bookish father to guess her namesake.

The lines came to her:
Shake off slumber, and beware:
Awake, awake.

She couldn't remember when in *The Tempest* Ariel uttered those lines, or to whom, or to what purpose. Still, the message was clear. It was a warning. She should get out of bed. Get away from Jacob. *The only way to break an addiction is to go cold turkey.* But what if she wasn't addicted? Or rather, what if she was addicted to Jacob—not like addicted to a drug, but like addicted to . . . water . . . light . . . air.

What are you saying? Ariel asked herself. *Are you saying you need Jacob Hunter? That Jacob Hunter is essential to sustaining your life?* The thought was scarier than thinking she was just hooked on having sex with him. Though while she was in the admitting frame of mind, she might as well come clean with herself—she *was* hooked on the sex. She was a total goner. Jacob had brought her to climax three times over the course of the night and she was still hungry for more.

Sighing, Ariel surrendered to her impulses. She snuggled closer to him and even in his sleep he tightened his arms around her protectively. He murmured something and Ariel pressed her ear to his chest. The low rumble of his voice soothed her. His tone was gentle. What had he said?

"I love you," Jacob whispered. Ariel froze. She wasn't sure if she'd heard correctly. Was he awake? Asleep? Ariel lie breathing against him for what felt like hours before she drifted off again into dreams.

She woke again with light streaming around her. Jacob had rolled onto his side. He regarded her with a devilishly sexy smile, trailing his knuckles between her breasts, heading down to her navel . . . and lower . . . Ariel caught his hand.

"I think we need to talk," she said.

His grin widened. "First we need to build more trust," he said.

In the sober light of day, Ariel felt more detached from her grand pronouncements of the night before. The night before . . . when she'd basically told Jacob Hunter she had unshakeable, eternal faith in him based on nothing but a feeling. Sheesh. She was getting too mystic for her own good. Well, maybe a slight amendment was in order.

*

"Talking is essential to trust," said Ariel definitively. "Honest conversation? Ring any bells?"

Jacob shook his head. Ariel could be such a know it all. Stubborn. Infuriating. He loved to tease her and watch her bristle. He loved the moment when, invariably, her defenses broke down and he saw her realize the absurdity of her position. Of his position. Of everything.

She was a woman who took her job seriously. That much was obvious to anyone. But he'd learned over the past few days that she didn't take herself seriously. Or at least, not so seriously that she couldn't laugh at herself. He loved her sense of humor, her ability to spar with him. He found it very, very sexy.

"Building trust is physical," said Jacob with a straight face. Ariel raised an eyebrow. "That's what you were getting at last night. I mean, that's what you were getting *to*. The physical aspect of trust."

"Physical," she echoed.

"Physical," said Jacob. "When people want to build trust they go to a ropes course. They practice falling into each other's arms. Trust is basic. It's about bodies . . . interacting . . . in the most . . . basic . . . way . . . "

*

With every word, he moved his hands over her skin. He pulled the sheet down from her legs and exposed more of her bare flesh. A finger brushed her clitoris.

"Basic?" Ariel asked. She arched up to meet his kiss and dragged him across her. His full weight pressed her into the mattress. "If we're going to build trust *physically*," she said, "I want you to know I'm tired of the basics." She could feel him smiling against her shoulder. She couldn't help but cry out as his fingers moved between her legs.

"Are we moving on to Advanced Trust?" asked Jacob. "Are you sure you're ready for that?" His finger slid inside her. She moaned, tried to writhe beneath him, but his weight pinned her.

"You have to be willing to be completely vulnerable," he whispered. She was breathing against his neck, hands twisting in his hair, as his fingers stroked her. "You have to be willing to let go. Absolutely. No inhibitions. No fear." With one hand, he caught her beneath the knees. He turned her over and pulled her hips toward him. Ariel gasped. She was on her knees, her legs spread, her back arched. She felt so exposed. But she was excited by the new position. It felt daring, shameless.

With a slow stroke, he drove himself into her.

"Jacob," she moaned as his length filled her, the angle allowing him to press deeper than she'd ever imagined possible. The waves of pleasure were already crashing through her, starting from the center of her being and washing in electric ripples to the very tips of her fingers and toes. "Oh, god, wait, oh, please" she was crying out, half mortified that the pleasure had taken her so soon.

"Let go, darling," he whispered. "Let go." A hand reached around her waist to caress her from the front as he moved into and out of her warm, moist cleft from behind. She began to buck and sob.

And then she absolutely let go.

By the time Ariel opened her eyes again, the light slanting through the window was making a rectangle in the far corner of the room. She had no idea what time it was. She couldn't believe how many times Jacob had made love to her in the past twelve hours. She tried to count on her fingers.

"Don't tally yet," came Jacob's deep voice. "I think I have a little more left in me."

Ariel chuckled sheepishly. He was alert, awake, propped up on an elbow, giving her a smoldering look. Even before having coffee, his wits were quick. He'd seen her counting and had immediately inferred what she was doing.

"I believe you," she said, blushing. Then she gave him a coy glance. "That's why I love endurance athletes," she joked. She sat up, climbed out of bed. She held the sheet loosely around her breasts, suddenly shy in the morning light. Of course, that meant that Jacob was left completely uncovered. He didn't care a bit. He crossed his arms behind his head and looked up at her. *He* was the one with the breathtaking body. But as he looked at her admiration glowed in his eyes.

*

"I'm hungry," Ariel pronounced. "I want breakfast." She squirmed into a light silk chemise and stood for a moment in the patch of sun. Jacob felt the blood rush to his penis as he stared at her, the silk clinging to her curves, her hair spilling like sunrise over her creamy shoulders. He thought about dragging the bedspread around his hips, but it was too late. His arousal was on display. Ariel's gaze dropped to his impressively swollen girth and her mouth dropped open.

"What?" he said innocently. "I *am* an endurance athlete."

"We need food to fuel all this endurance," said Ariel, taking the room service menu from her desk and crawling back onto the bed. She flopped on her stomach, the menu in front of her.

"Pancakes?" she asked. Jacob stroked the small of her back.

"Tell me, Ariel Hayes," he said. "What did you mean when you said, 'I *love* endurance athletes?'"

Ariel glanced at him. His tone was casual. The joking light still danced in his eyes. Ariel licked her lips. "I was extrapolating," she said. "Bacon? Or sausage?"

"How many endurance athletes have you loved?" Jacob persisted. He sat up.

Ariel's gaze traveled immediately to his chest, his stomach. "Hash browns?" she said slowly, brow furrowed.

Jacob didn't want to drop his line of questioning. It had suddenly occurred to him that maybe Ariel Hayes, journalist with *Cycling Today*, had slept with her interviewees before.

Was he jealous? It would be crazy to be jealous of things Ariel might have done before she'd even *met* him. Still, he couldn't shake the thought of her in bed with other . . . *endurance athletes*. He had to know.

"Am I the first person you've profiled so . . . personally?" he asked.

Ariel let the menu drop. "I know I haven't given you much of a reason to believe in my professionalism," she said, "but I assure you this behavior . . . " She indicated the disordered hotel room . . . the clothing flung here and there . . . "Is highly irregular."

"Who else have you profiled?" Jacob asked. "Come on. Tell me."

He was keeping his tone light, joking, but then Ariel hesitated, and he knew his assumption was correct. "You *have* gotten personal with other cyclists," he breathed. "Is this a pattern for you?"

"Jacob," Ariel snapped. "You're being ridiculous. Of course I haven't slept with other cyclists. I don't sleep with the people I write articles about. It's unethical. It's more than unethical—it's messy and it's stupid and it leads to situations like this." She got up and stalked to the window.

"Why won't you tell me about your other articles?" he asked. "If your relationships with those other guys were so professional?" He hated the whining quality in his voice. He was behaving poorly, and he knew it. Acting like a jealous adolescent. Part of him wanted to stop. He wanted to drop the whole thing and order a stack of blueberry pancakes. What could be better than lying in bed with Ariel, eating blueberry pancakes?

"Who did you write your last article about?" he heard himself saying. "Do I know him?"

"Jacob," Ariel said in a strange tone of voice. She was looking out the window.

"Let's see," said Jacob. With a lithe motion, he rose from the bed and pulled on a pair of boxer briefs. He sat down at the desk where her laptop was open, the screen dark, sleeping. Jacob tapped the space bar.

"We'll do this the old-fashioned way," he said.

"What are you talking about?" asked Ariel. She took a step toward him. The expression on her face triggered alarm bells in Jacob's mind. He brought up her web browser.

"I'm going to Google you, Ariel Hayes," he said.

"Google me?" said Ariel dully.

Jacob's eyes glinted. "Yes, Google you," he said in an exaggeratedly didactic voice. "In our grandparents' time, suitors depended on the web to gather information about their sweethearts. Of course, the web wasn't based on computers connected through fiber-optic cables. It was usually a little more local. You had to rely on town gossips. But it was every bit as effective. Don't have any illusions about progress."

He typed "Ariel Hayes" and pressed search.

"Jacob," Ariel began. But it was too late. The hits were back.

"*X-Ray*," said Jacob. He clicked on the first result and looked at the screen uncomprehendingly. "What is this?" he asked, scrolling down. One thing was clear. It wasn't *Cycling Today*.

"There's something I have to tell you," Ariel said, voice catching.

Jacob pushed back his chair and faced her with fury in his eyes.

"I don't write for *Cycling Today*," she said.

"The Internet is way ahead of your confession," he said, his voice dripping scorn. "Tell me about *X-Ray*."

"It's a small New York-based magazine," she said. "Mostly political. Unflinching exposés. Social and political issues."

"So assuming you sleep with all of your subjects, you've slept with more senators than cyclists," said Jacob. His voice was hard.

"I don't sleep with my subjects." Ariel's voice cracked. "I've never done anything like this before. I didn't want to come here. I didn't want to write this article." She raked her hands desperately through her hair. Her agitation caused her eyes to shine. A becoming flush stained her cheeks. Her breasts rose and fell temptingly in the silk chemise. Jacob commanded himself to remain unmoved. To steel himself against any sympathy. She had lied to him. She wasn't writing a celebrity profile for a cycling magazine. She was writing a different kind of article, for a different kind of magazine.

"Exactly what article are you writing, Ariel?" asked Jacob.

*

Ariel reached toward him but he ignored her proffered hand. Instead, he picked his shirt off the carpet and pulled it over his head.

"I'm supposed to write an article exposing you for using performance-enhancing drugs," Ariel whispered. "But I'm not going to do it. I've been wanting to tell you, but I haven't known how."

Jacob was pulling on his jeans. She wanted to throw her arms around him but she knew he wouldn't let her. He was seething and she couldn't blame him. She'd lied to him. But he hadn't been entirely honest with her, either.

"Tell me why you had meth in your hotel room," said Ariel. "I'm sure there's an explanation. I trust you. Just tell me, please.

Jacob finished dressing. He strode to Ariel, standing so that their bodies were only an inch apart. The air between them felt superheated.

"I am not going to tell you anything," Jacob whispered. "You have your story now. You have what you came for. I wouldn't dream of taking that away from you. I know how important your career is to you. I know you don't care what lives you destroy to get what you want. So please," he stepped back, bowing slightly. An ironic bow that cut her to ribbons. "Please," he said, "do what you will with the fruits of your labor. Write your article. The truth must come out, right? It seems like you came to Colorado with your mind made up about what that is."

Ariel started to speak but he'd already turned away from her. The door slammed behind him. Ariel collapsed on the bed in a storm of weeping she knew wouldn't end for a long, long time.

Chapter Thirteen

Brian Jenks gunned his truck's engine, accelerating as he pulled off the street to park in front of the gated rehab center. He liked to see dust rising in his rearview mirror. He jumped down to the pavement, slammed the heavy door. He tucked his faded Nuggets t-shirt into his jeans, threw his baseball cap through the open driver's side window, and ran a hand through his hair. Tidying up. No good looking like a derelict in a rehab center, for Christ's sake. He put on his humble little twelve-step smile.

Yes, I've found my higher power, thank you very much, you sanctimonious bastards.

He was buzzed through the gate and walked up the short path to the porch. No matter how hard he tried to disguise it for the benefit of these nurses—busybody teetotalers and Jesus freaks—he couldn't deny that he was in a thundering rage. Meeting with the journalist with the sexy voice was his opportunity to tell his side of the story. To tell the world what he thought of Jacob Hunter. To rub some dirt in that handsome, arrogant face. He had a pack of wild tales saved up for the occasion. All a little less than accurate. But that was what the media was all about, right? Serving up a pack of lies on a platter. Causing trouble, ruining lives. Jacob Hunter's life was the one Brian would most like to ruin right now. Pretty-boy Jake had come close to ruining his.

He'd had a good thing going with Karen. She was smoking hot, with her long blond hair and sexy body. Sexy until she lost so much weight. When Karen started to look strung out, Brian began to look for kicks elsewhere. But there were other reasons to keep her around.

She kept the house clean, right up until the end. When she was high, she'd spend all night washing, scrubbing, mopping. Brian liked a tidy house. Just didn't like doing the work himself.

She didn't talk back, either. Not, that is, after he'd shown her what the consequences of backtalk could be.

Best of all, she listened to him. Like no one ever had before. Brian could tell her anything and she'd sit quietly, listening with an expression of concern and tenderness in her big hazel eyes. Concern for him. Love. He could talk about the things he couldn't with anyone else. Who was she going to tell, anyway? He'd let her know early on he didn't like her seeing friends without him around. Didn't like her going to see her family. He knew the Hunters hated him. He knew they'd fill up her head with their snobbish notions, their proud nonsense about education and careers. All the education a woman needed, Brian thought gloatingly, he was more than qualified to provide. And he knew exactly in what form it was most effectively delivered.

Jake took Karen away from him. Shut her up in a cage. Poisoned her mind. Made her look at Brian with suspicion, with mistrust. But Brian wasn't going to let Jake win. He was going to keep Karen. The presents he delivered to her in the hospital ensured she'd stay by his side. Connected. Tied. Just the way he wanted.

He had another one for her today, tucked in a secret pocket sewn into the lining of his bomber jacket. Useful for run-ins with the police, or for situations like this one. The nurses—or jailers, as he liked to call them—thought they were clever. They made him turn out his pockets every time he came. But they never caught on to him.

He jerked his head, cracking his neck, and bounced a few times on his toes. Cool and collected. Ready for action. He stepped into the house, ready for Bettina's inspection.

The dark-haired nurse came out of her office as he entered. Brian expected the usual pleasant greeting. When it suited his purposes, Brian knew he could be one charming SOB. He'd made sure to butter up Bettina at every opportunity. Women were so simple. Tell them they had pretty eyes, a nice dress on, bring them flowers once in a while—they thought you were a goddamn prince.

Bettina didn't look so friendly today, even after Brian delivered the devilish, crooked grin that usually had her swooning. Even after he'd drawled her name, slow and husky, and asked her how she was doing. Without smiling, to Brian's complete shock, she told him sternly, "You can't see Karen today, Mr. Jenks."

Brian stepped back, surprised. Recovering, he asked: "Can I see her tomorrow, then?"

Bettina shook her head. "She's requested that you not be allowed to visit, Mr. Jenks. She and her brother both. For the rest of her stay here. I'm sorry, but I'll have to ask you to leave . . . and please, respect their wishes. Don't come back."

Brian took a moment to process what Bettina had told him. As it sunk in, he came forward, locking her eyes with his own. He hissed at her, "Now look, woman. Karen's my girlfriend. You can't make me believe she don't want to see me. She loves me. This is some sick scheme you and that bastard brother of hers cooked up between you. I'm not falling for it. If she don't want me around, she's gonna have to tell me that herself. I got a right to see her."

Holding her ground, Bettina told him, "Actually, Mr. Jenks, you have no rights in this situation. Only immediate family members are guaranteed visitation privileges. Even those can be suspended at the request of the patient. It doesn't matter whether or not you believe me, but Karen told me herself that she didn't want to see you anymore. That you were bad for her recovery. Her brother was there, yes, but she made the decision."

The security guard came down the hallway then, and seeing Brian's aggressive stance, picked up his pace and jogged the rest of the way down the hall. Bettina stepped back. "This gentleman will escort you outside. Goodbye, Mr. Jenks."

Brian looked to either side of him. He was a big man, but the security guard loomed over him, and had the width to match his height. Grinding his teeth, he glared for a moment longer at Bettina, looked down the hallway toward Karen's door . . . then turned on his heel and marched out, tailed by the guard.

*

Brian retreated to the shelter of his trailer on the outskirts of Leadville. What he wanted to do—more than anything—was to find Jacob Hunter. To break his face so thoroughly no woman would ever look at him again. Then to break his legs, so he'd never be able to get back on that bicycle of his, either.

Brian spent hours nursing a twelve-pack of Coors, then a bottle of bourbon. He imagined Jacob broken, destroyed, bleeding on the ground in front of him. He relished that image, turning it over and over in his mind as his vision began to blur from the liquor. The drunker he got, the more certain he was that another fight between him and Jacob Hunter would come out differently than the last one, that he'd be the one wiping the sidewalk with Jacob's face, instead of the other way around. He was just about ready to climb into his truck and peal out of the driveway, to teach Hunter the lesson that was coming to him. Then he passed out in his chair.

In the morning, with a splitting hangover and a sore neck from his night sleeping propped upright, Brian's confidence was less solid. He couldn't forget the nightmare of seeing Hunter standing victoriously over him while he felt cold concrete against his cheek and warm blood running into his eyes from the split skin on his brow. It had taken him a week to recover from that fight. He'd sat in his living room, raw steak draped over his matching shiners, dreaming of revenge.

He hadn't felt certain of his ability to take Hunter down then, either. As much as it sickened him to admit it, he suspected that he might not be able to beat Hunter in a fair fight, man to man.

But he did still have a shot at pulling him down. Something that didn't involve a direct confrontation.

He was going to find Ariel Hayes. And he was going to dish some dirt on Jacob that would make her skin crawl. A combination of truth and lies. He'd tell her about Karen. Get back at her for betraying him. He'd make the whole Hunter clan sorry for the way they'd discounted him, closed ranks against him. But he wouldn't stop there. He was willing to perjure himself to bring down Jacob Hunter. He'd tell her that squeaky-clean Jacob had done things Brian knew the uptight bastard wouldn't have been able to imagine in his wildest dreams.

It didn't matter if it was true. It just mattered that *she* believed him. She didn't even have to believe him. She just had to want a story that would sell magazines.

*

When Brian entered the lobby of the Alpenhof Hotel that evening he almost choked. It was the kind of place designed to make a man who'd made little money all his life, who'd lived on the outskirts of society, feel a combination of envy and hate.

Smoothing the emotion from his face, he strolled casually to the reception desk and smiled a charming smile at the young woman behind the desk. She returned his smile warmly.

"Darlin'," Brian drawled, leaning on his elbows, "I need to find Ariel Hayes. She's a guest here. We had an appointment yesterday, and I stood her up. I want to apologize. Tell me what room she's staying in, and I'll go on up there and do that."

"Sorry, sir, I can't tell you her room number," the receptionist said, batting her eyelashes at him, "but I can call her room and ask if she wants you to come up."

Brian stifled a twinge of uneasiness. What if she wouldn't see him? But he answered, "Go ahead and do that. Hope she's not too mad." He winked at the pretty girl, who blushed as she picked up the telephone.

As she dialed, the receptionist's eyes scanned the lobby. To Brian's surprise, she hung up before the phone could have even rung. Pointing behind Brian's shoulder, she whispered confidentially,

"I'm not supposed to do this. But she's right over there. You can go ahead and talk to her."

Brian turned to see where the girl was pointing. To his intense satisfaction, he saw that she'd indicated a stunning redheaded woman in a linen dress and sandals. She was staring at a map, frowning. As he approached, Brian took advantage of her distraction to look her up and down unabashedly. She was hot stuff, all right. Long legs, curvaceous, vivid coloring. Brian imagined how her hair would look hanging down around her naked, pink-tipped breasts, and it almost gave him a hard-on.

"Ariel Hayes?" he asked smoothly.

*

Ariel jerked, startled by the nearness of the man she hadn't noticed approaching. She looked up at him, frowning. She'd had an overwhelming day. One that had started off well, only to get very, very bad. After Jacob had left her room, she'd cried for what seemed like hours. She was certain that her face was splotchy, puffy, that the pain in her eyes was telecasting to everyone who looked at her.

She'd just screwed things up with the one man she'd ever opened to fully . . . body and mind. She wanted to stay in her hotel room and weep forever. She'd finally decided to go for a drive, try to find that stretch of highway Jacob had taken her to when they'd escaped from the sponsor's party. Getting somewhere outdoors where she could be all alone, under the sky.

That was what she needed right now. Not chatting up some guy in the hotel lobby. She didn't know who he was. But she knew she didn't have the energy to deal with him. She let her gaze drift away and started to walk toward the exit.

"I'm Brian Jenks," he said in a richly modulated, unctuous voice that Ariel mistrusted. This guy clearly thought he was a charmer. Maybe young girls from small town Colorado would be taken in. But though she was from a small town herself, Ariel had spent too many years in New York City to fall for a smooth presentation. She was a reporter who'd seen it all . . . or so she'd liked to think. She sighed internally, knowing she wasn't as hard-boiled as all that. She was barely *soft*-boiled. She was a runny mess.

"What is it?" she asked warily.

"I was sorry to miss you yesterday," Brian said, leaning forward. "Maybe we got our signals crossed. I was hoping I could take you out to dinner. I'd like to give you that interview. I have some things to fill you in on . . . let's just say I think you'll find it worth your while. Illuminating, if you will."

Ariel took a step back, increasing the space between her body and Brian's to a width she was comfortable with. "I'm sorry," she said in what she hoped was a neutral tone. "I'm no longer looking for that type of information. The story will probably be canceled. If not, I've gotten all the material I need from Jacob himself."

"And you trust him?" Brian asked, trying to keep his voice even. "Surely you can see he's got something to hide. And I can tell, you it's not pretty."

Ariel shook her head. "I'm really not interested," she said flatly. "And I have to go. I'm late to meet someone."

"Oh, really," Brian said, his eyes narrowing, "like you were *late* to meet me yesterday? You probably shouldn't bother showing up at all."

Ariel frowned. Brian's tone was suddenly hostile. She hadn't felt good about wasting his time the day before. But she was quickly growing to dislike him enough that she didn't care.

"I'm sorry I wasn't able to keep our appointment yesterday," she told him, "but something came up. Something unavoidable. I'm no longer interested in meeting with you. And I do have to leave now. Goodbye, Mr. Jenks." She turned to walk past him toward the front doors.

Brian reached out and grabbed her arm, hard, as she tried to sweep past him, pulling her around so they were face to face again.

Ariel turned white with shock, then flushed red with anger.

"You need to know this," he told her, not realizing he was yelling, that people were starting to stare. "The world needs to know this. It's your job to tell them."

"Let. Go. Of. Me." Ariel pulled away, wincing as Brian's fingers dug into her arm. Her pale skin bruised easily. She was sure he'd leave marks. She didn't like the idea of having any trace of this man left on her. She found him repellant. And now, quite frightening.

"It's not my job to publish whatever some lowlife scum decides he wants to see in print. Stop yelling, and leave me alone." She pulled harder away from him, and Brian jerked her back toward him, so that she stumbled and fell against him, her hair whipping around her face.

"Bitch!" Brian yelled, one hand digging into her arm, the other buried in her hair, pulling her head back painfully. "I'm scum, am I? Your precious Jacob tell you that?" He bent his head to plant a brutal, punishing kiss on Ariel's unwilling lips.

His mouth never touched hers. A tremendous blow delivered to the side of his head sent him careening to the floor. At the same moment, Ariel was snatched from his grasp and she found herself pulled into Jacob's familiar embrace.

"Ariel," Jacob whispered into her ear, holding her tight against him. "Are you all right? Did he hurt you?"

A tight lump formed in her throat as relief washed through her—not just to be freed from Brian's appalling grasp, but to be safe in Jacob's arms, when she'd thought he'd never touch her again. She shook her head. "No, no, I'm fine. Just get him out of here."

*

Jacob released Ariel and turned resolutely to Brian, who was staggering unsteadily to his feet. He grabbed him by the collar and dragged him, stumbling, out the front door. Once they were outside, he pulled Brian to his feet, stepped back, and punched him again, in the jaw, as hard as he could. Brian reeled backwards and fell to the pavement, a trickle of blood running from his split lip.

"The first one was for Ariel," Jacob said grimly. "That one's for Karen. If I ever see your face again, I won't stop at two. Don't come anywhere near me, near Ariel, near anyone in my family. Ever again." He turned on his heel and walked back into the hotel, leaving Brian Jenks bleeding and stunned on the sidewalk.

When he got back to Ariel, who was still working to calm her breathing, he wrapped his arms around her again. She collapsed gratefully into his arms.

"Jacob," she said, her voice trembling with emotion, "I'm so sorry I lied to you . . . so sorry . . . "

"Hey there," Jacob whispered her, burying his lips in her hair, his heart brimming. "Don't worry. Don't worry. It doesn't matter. All that matters is that you're safe." He kissed her forehead. "Let's go home."

*

Ariel nodded. She expected him to turn her toward the elevators, to take her back to his room or her own. Instead, to her surprise, he put his arm tenderly around her shoulders and led her to the doors of the lobby.

When they exited the hotel, Brian Jenks was gone. The valet had pulled Jacob's motorcycle up to the curb, leaving the keys in the ignition and the engine running.

"C'mon, love," Jacob said gently. The tenderness in his voice sent a shiver of disbelieving pleasure down Ariel's spine. "We're going home."

He climbed onto the motorcycle and Ariel straddled the bike after him. Together, they roared off into the night, toward Leadville.

Chapter Fourteen

As Jacob leaned into the curves of the road, Ariel learned with him, surrendering to the rushing wind. They were traveling up and up, to an even higher elevation. The air felt cool on Ariel's arms. Sometimes the roar of the motorcycle faded out as her ears popped with the pressure.

When their pace began to slacken, she shifted her weight slightly and lifted her head to look around. They were still outside of Leadville. The guardrails were rusted. Cows were grazing on either side of the road, roaming between the stanchions of the power lines. They passed a trailer park, several of the trailers decorated with massive antlers. Mule deer? Elk? She'd like to see an elk. Maybe Jacob could take her into the mountains one day. He must know places people could go to see elk. And big horn sheep! She imaged hiking with him in September, walking beneath a shivering golden dome of aspen leaves as he pointed out the sheep clambering among red boulders.

Don't get ahead of yourself.

As they rode into Leadville, she thought she'd never seen a place so wildly beautiful and so remote, so ravaged and desolate. She smelled tar, saw torn up earth from mining operations, little shacks no bigger than their propane tanks, and heaps of old, blackened machinery with functions she couldn't imagine. Jacob Hunter was a living testament to all of it: the good and the bad. This was the town that made him who he was today.

As they entered the center of town, Jacob drove slowly. It was even more like something out of a Wild West movie than Minturn. Ariel craned her neck to gawk at the Tabor Opera House. Ha! Finally. There was her opera house. She wondered if there had been ballets during mining times, when Leadville had enjoyed the silver boom that put so many Colorado towns on the map. Probably not. She imagined spirited burlesque singers: daring women with boots and lacy bustiers, waving feathered fans at crowds of hooting men. She imagined herself in tall leather boots and garters, dancing for Jacob on a spotlit stage. She couldn't help but giggle.

She wondered if she would ever dance for Jacob. For the first time in years, the idea didn't cause her pain. There'd been so much frustration and pain knotted up with the very idea of dancing. Now she thought maybe she'd like to whirl around and around, to feel her body moving through a series of unrehearsed, exuberant arabesques.

Silver Dollar Saloon. Masonic Temple. National Mining Hall of Fame. Ariel wanted to explore it all. But not tonight. Jacob turned, and soon the buildings became fewer, more spread out. They were shabbier in appearance, less maintained. The larger buildings seemed abandoned, or at the least, not residential. There was a mixture of private homes, maintained yards, little stretches of brush and grass, industrial blight.

Ariel let her gaze wander up past the housetops. She could see snowcapped mountains in the distance. They were breathtaking. What an odd place to grow up. She decided she loved Leadville.

By the time Jacob pulled into the driveway of a small, neat bungalow, her cheeks were glowing. She hopped off the bike, took off the helmet, and shook out her hair. Jacob sat on the bike, watching her with a strange expression.

"What?" she said, suddenly self-conscious.

"You're stunning," he said simply. Ariel couldn't hold his gaze. The intensity in his golden eyes took away her power of speech. She turned away from him and gazed off at the beauty of the horizon.

"*This* is stunning," Ariel said. "All of this. The air. The mountains. They're covered in snow!"

"Mt. Elbert and Mt. Massive," said a warm voice. A slight woman with graying blond hair and kind brown eyes had opened the front door of the bungalow. She looked familiar. She looked like Jacob. Ariel could see where he'd gotten his bone structure and his coloring. This woman had to be his mother.

"Mrs. Hunter." Ariel smiled, extending her hand, but the woman bypassed the hand and instead, she gave Ariel a surprisingly strong hug. She smelled of cinnamon and apples.

"Beth," she said. "Call me Beth. And you must be Ariel. Jacob, somehow I must have known you were coming tonight."

Jacob hung his helmet from a handlebar and folded his mother in a bear hug. "You made pie," he crowed. He looked at Ariel, his face alight with boyish triumph. Seeing him with that boyish glee in his face, his arm around his mother's shoulders, made Ariel's eyes fill momentarily with tears.

"It's a talent I have," continued Jacob, oblivious to Ariel's sudden rush of emotion. "I can sense when Mom is baking. If I'm within a thousand miles, I make my way to the house before the pie comes out of the oven. Let me guess . . . "

"It came out of the oven five minutes ago," Beth finished her son's sentence and gave him a playful swat as he barreled through the front door.

"Don't touch," she called after him. "It has to cool."

Ariel stood in the little yard, alone with Beth Hunter. She fumbled around for something to say. "Your flowers are beautiful," she said shyly. "Are those Indian blankets?"

Beth nodded at the bed of cheerful orange flowers. "They are indeed," she said. She gave Ariel an appraising look. "Jacob told me you were gorgeous," she said, "but he also told me you were from New York City. I didn't think a girl from New York City would know the first thing about Colorado flowers."

Ariel blushed. Jacob had told his mother she was gorgeous? Jacob had talked to his mother about her?

"I'm not from New York City," she explained. "I'm from upstate. A small town. My mother used to have a beautiful garden. She planted Indian blanket and sunflowers and day lilies and cardinal flowers. All the red and orange flowers. She loved red and orange."

Maybe Beth noticed that Ariel had used the past tense. Her expression was tender. "Was your mother a redhead too?" she asked.

"Flaming," exclaimed Ariel. "Worse than me."

"You make it sound like a case of strep throat." Beth laughed.

"Spoken like a true school nurse," said Jacob. He'd emerged from the house. His voice sounded odd. As though he was talking with his mouth full . . .

"Are you eating my pie?" scolded Beth.

"I'm eating your oatmeal cookies," said Jacob. "Your pie is safe. Though you did leave it defenseless on the windowsill."

"I should have electrified it," muttered Beth, but Ariel could tell she was delighted. Delighted at every word that came out of Jacob's mouth . . . filled with her pie, or no. Delighted that he was there.

Ariel hadn't been around a mother, anyone's mother, in years. It made her heart ache, but she liked it. She liked Beth Hunter.

"We were just talking about Ariel's beautiful red hair," said Beth with a conspiratorial glance at Ariel. "I was hoping it was contagious."

Ariel followed Beth and Jacob into the house. She felt welcomed by Beth's kind, mirthful presence. Beth seemed to have accepted her instantly and Ariel was moved. Grateful.

"We already ate supper," Beth was saying to Jacob. "Your father is resting."

"I won't bother him," said Jacob. Then, to Ariel, "Let's go to the kitchen."

The kitchen was redolent with the smell of buttery pastry. Ariel and Jacob sat at the table while Beth bustled about, making tea.

"My mom likes you," whispered Jacob. He'd grabbed Ariel's hand under the table and Ariel felt a guilty thrill. "She has a good sense about people."

Ariel met Jacob's eyes. Maybe it wasn't the right time, but she couldn't resist. The day had been so traumatic. She couldn't just pretend nothing had happened. She needed to make things better. "I am so sorry I lied to you," she said. He tightened his grip on her hand, a comforting squeeze.

"You don't have to . . . " he began, but Ariel cut him off.

"It *was* just a story to me," she said. "An opportunity to write a thrilling article and make a name for myself. But as soon as I started to get to know you . . . " Her voice faltered and she dropped her eyes. " . . . to have feelings for you . . . I didn't want to write the story anymore. I didn't know what to do. How to tell you."

Beth twisted at the waist, still pouring water from the teakettle into two yellow mugs.

"It sounds like you two are having a serious discussion," she observed. "That calls for pie."

"But it's still cooling!" protested Ariel. Jacob frowned at her.

"Whose side are you on?" he grumbled.

"He's easier to deal with when he has his pie," explained Beth, putting a mug of chamomile tea in front of Ariel. "That's not to say *easy*. Easier."

"So for Ariel's sake, you'll let me have pie now? Thanks, I think," said Jacob. While Beth took the pie from the windowsill, Jacob took the opportunity to kiss Ariel gently on the lips.

"I overreacted," whispered Jacob. "I haven't treated you fairly, either. I've been riled up for weeks. Acting like an ass. When I saw Brian shaking you . . . " He shook his head darkly. "He's lucky he's alive."

Beth had started at the sound of Brian's name. "Brian?" she asked, and for the first time, Ariel heard a strained note in her warm voice. "Jake, what happened? Where did you see Brian?" Ariel's gaze dropped to her arm, the pale skin already darkening with shadowy bruises. Beth's gaze followed Ariel's.

"Jake, what happened tonight?" she asked, her voice more level.

"We'll talk later," said Jacob. He stood up and circled behind his mother, putting his hands on her shoulders and rubbing them with strong, comforting motions. She allowed her head to drop. After a moment, she reached up to lay her hands on his.

"We need to have a serious discussion, Jake," she said.

Jacob kissed the top her head.

"With plenty of pie," he said.

"Is it a two piece conversation?" asked Beth, the sparkle returning to her eyes.

"Yeah," said Jacob, "maybe three."

Beth whistled. "That bad, huh?"

"It's bad," Jacob confirmed. He sat back down next to Ariel at the kitchen table. He looked at her for a long moment, then looked back at his mother.

"But I think things are getting better," he said. He grinned that cocky, heart-stopping grin. "I *know* things are getting better."

Beth cut a piece of pie and levered it from the pan. She put it on a plate, the golden wedge steaming and fragrant, the apples spilling from the crust.

"Give it to Ariel," said Jacob as Beth put the piece in front of him on the table.

Beth suppressed a smile as she pushed the plate to Ariel. "My dear, I think he likes you," she said. Jacob jumped up to get Ariel a fork.

Ariel took a bite of pie. It tasted like autumn in heaven. She beamed at Beth. "He *does* like me," she said. "I didn't understand until I tasted this pie, but now I get it. This is the best thing I've ever eaten."

"I wouldn't give up the first piece to just anyone," said Jacob.

His eyes followed his mother's every movement as she cut another piece of pie.

"Thank you," he said, attacking the pie with an eagerness that made Beth and Ariel smile.

"I should bring a piece to your father," said Beth.

"I'll do it," offered Ariel.

Jacob looked at her in surprise.

Beth simply nodded. "That would be nice," she said. "He's looking forward to meeting you."

Ariel entered the dark living room with hesitant steps. A shadowy form stirred in the corner.

"You can turn on the light," said a deep baritone. "It's on your left." Ariel flipped the switch. Jacob's father sat in the armchair near the couch. He was a powerfully built man, still handsome, with thick brown hair and a chiseled face. Ariel could tell just by looking at him that he must have been extremely strong in his youth. She knew from Jacob that he still hadn't come to terms with losing his sight. She couldn't imagine what it would be like to go blind. To never see the faces of the people she loved ever again. She knew, though, what it was like to lose people she loved. She'd never see her mother or her father ever again, or hear their voices, or feel the touch of their hands. She wondered if the Hunters understood how lucky they were.

"I wanted to bring you a piece of pie," said Ariel, "before Jacob ate the whole thing. I'm Ariel Hayes. I'm . . . a friend of Jacob's," she finished, feeling the blush spread across her face as she tripped over her words.

Her stutter had raised the ghost of a smile on Jacob's father's lips. He put out his hand and Ariel balanced the fork across the plate and placed it on his palm. As he fixed his grip on the plate, Ariel looked at the walls. They were covered in family photos. Jacob in a blue snowsuit, tufts of white-blond hair escaping from his woolen hat. Jacob leaping into a swimming hole, his legs almost painfully thin.

Ariel watched him grow up from picture to picture. His hair turned to a darker blond, his chest filled out, his legs thickened with muscle. That grin, though, it stayed the same from picture to picture, year to year. Infuriating. Irresistible. Ariel moved closer to look at the chubby blond child that appeared with Jacob by the Christmas tree. The little girl with blond ringlets in the party hat. The beautiful, somber teenager posed on a low stone wall for her yearbook portrait.

Jacob had never mentioned a sister.

Ariel heard footsteps behind her. Beth and Jacob had come into the room. Beth moved to sit on the side of the couch nearest her husband. Jacob put his arms around Ariel's waist.

"That's my sister Karen," he said. He guided Ariel to the couch and, there, sitting with the Hunters, she heard the whole story. Jacob talked for over an hour, filling Ariel in on Karen's battle with addiction. Some of the more recent events were clearly new to Jacob's parents—Ariel saw Richard clench his hands into fists when Jacob talked about finding drugs in Karen's hospital room.

"What kind of place are they running?" he burst out.

"How would you know?" retorted Jacob. "Have you ever visited?" The words snapped like a whip-crack. Jacob's father flinched.

"That's not fair, Jacob," said Beth, quietly. "Don't be cruel."

Jacob's father had turned away. Now he turned his face back toward his son. His face was pale. "So I should show up? Go to the hospital?" he asked. "With my cane? Remind Karen how tough her life is? That her father is . . ."

"What, Dad?" said Jacob. From the urgency his tone, Ariel could tell that this exchange was a long time in coming. "That her father is what?" said Jacob. "Blind? That her father is blind? We can say it, right? We have to say it. To face it. *Blind.*"

"*Useless,*" Jacob's father burst out. "That her father is useless." He half-rose from his chair, his voice shaking with emotion.

"Goddamn useless." He threw himself back into his chair. The room fell silent. Beth reached out and put a hand on her husband's arm. He didn't move, didn't shrug her off.

"We love you, Richard," she said. "We love you and we need you."

"You're not useless, Dad," said Jacob. But he sounded defeated. Lost.

This wasn't Ariel's family. It would be bold to speak. But for the second time that evening, she felt like she had to say her part.

"My father used to tell me he felt useless, too," she said. Everyone turned at the sound of her voice. Her voice was trembling, but she kept going. Beth's expression comforted her. Jacob had put his head in his hands.

"He was in the car," said Ariel. "My father was in the car with my mother when they were hit by a drunk driver. My father was okay, but my mother died. She died at the scene. There was nothing my father could do. After it happened, I didn't speak for months. I hardly ate. My father didn't know how to help me. He couldn't help me. I was his little girl and I was suffering. And he couldn't take away the pain." Ariel took a deep breath. Jacob had raised his head. Slowly, he drew her hand into his lap. Caressed her palm. His golden eyes shone.

"When I was at Julliard and had to have foot surgery, he came to New York City," continued Ariel. "I couldn't stop crying. My dream of being a professional ballerina had shattered. I felt like everything was over. My father didn't heal my foot. He didn't even pick the right things to say. He kept trying to comfort me with Shakespeare quotes about fate. It was actually a disaster. He made me so angry I threw him out. I made him go to the Natural History Museum." Ariel laughed. Again, the faint smile ghosted Jacob's father's lips.

"But you know," said Ariel, "even though my father couldn't *do* anything to help me, he wasn't useless. He wasn't useless because he was *there*. That's all that mattered."

Jacob was fingering the bracelet on Ariel's wrist. She felt him touching the charms and smiled.

"I lost my father years ago," she said. "I miss him every day. But he's *still* not useless. Even now. Just thinking about him gives me the strength to go on."

"So what you're saying is this, and stop me if I'm wrong," said Jacob's father. He'd leaned forward in his chair again. Was he offended? Had she overstepped her role? Ariel felt a wave of anxiety. Jacob's father was a proud man. What if he interpreted her heartfelt speech as some kind of lecture? He rubbed his hands together as though thinking.

"What it boils down to is plain as apple pie," he said. "If your father can still make a difference in your life and he's dead, I can make a difference in my daughter's life while I'm alive and kicking. Even if I can't see my way straight to aim a kick at Brian Jenks's jaw."

"That's exactly what I'm saying," cried Ariel, relieved.

"You've got a son to kick Brian Jenks in the jaw, Pop," said Jacob. "We can delegate responsibilities."

"Let's not have any more kicking," said Beth. "Jacob, you could have been arrested."

"But I wasn't," said Jacob. "And now Karen is safe. She can recover without Brian trying to screw up her life. She can get back on her feet."

"How is the training going?" asked Jacob's father, and Jacob brightened at the question.

"Awesome," he said, and launched into a description of his training schedule so detailed that the next thing Ariel knew, she was being lifted off the couch and held against Jacob's wide chest. The house was completely dark. How many hours had passed?

"What . . ." she murmured.

"You fell asleep," said Jacob. "I should have known you never worked for *Cycling Today*. I'd barely said the word 'training' and it was lights out."

Toni Jones

"It's not that I'm not interested in your training," said Ariel, slapping his chest. "I've had a long day."

"I know," said Jacob gently. He carried her down the narrow hall.

"This used to be my bedroom," he said. "Now it's a guest room." He deposited Ariel onto the double bed.

"It's late and my parents asked us to stay. My mom wants to make her internationally acclaimed raspberry buckwheat pancakes for you in the morning. Do you mind?"

"I don't have anything to sleep in," said Ariel and Jacob's eyes glinted.

"It's your *childhood* room," said Ariel.

Jacob sat beside her on the bed. The humor vanished from his eyes. "Thank you, Ariel," he said. "For talking to my parents. For being here. For being you."

"I'm glad to be here," said Ariel. "I thought I'd lost you. This morning, I thought I'd lost you."

He pulled her against him and showed her it wasn't true.

The next morning, over raspberry buckwheat pancakes, Ariel laughed and chatted with Jacob's parents. She felt like she was a part of something. A part of a family. It was almost too good to be true. When she climbed onto the motorcycle behind Jacob and waved goodbye to Beth, the uneasy feeling increased. Every foot that she and Jacob descended down the mountain seemed to make the weight on her shoulders heavier.

Jacob's teasing words of the previous evening came back to her. *I should have known you never worked for* Cycling Today. *I'd barely said the word "training" and it was lights out.*

He'd been joking, but there was an element of truth to his words. She didn't know anything about cycling. And cycling was Jacob Hunter's life. Cycling took him to Italy, France, and Spain. It took him all around the world. Away from her. Panic rippled through Ariel's body.

She needed to call Theo. She needed to back out of the article. Her career was in shambles. But could she really let herself believe that Jacob Hunter was any kind of alternative? By the time they arrived at the Alpenhof, Ariel could barely breathe. Why was she so upset? It must be the intensity of the past few days combined with spending the night at the Hunters'. Getting to know Jacob's family. Wanting to belong so much it nearly killed her.

Because she couldn't have it. Not if she admitted the truth to herself. It was an impossible dream. Jacob seemed to care about her, but he was kidding himself, too. It would never work.

"Are you okay?" Jacob asked her as they walked into the lobby.

"I . . . " began Ariel.

"Fratello!" called Jacob.

"Jake, where have you been?" called Steve, running over to them. "Hi, Ariel." He gave her a brief smile. "Listen, you already missed your morning ride. We held the van for you and everything. Coach is pissed. You better get ready for sprints. You haven't won this race yet, you know."

"I'm ready," said Jacob. "Just tell the guys to wait. I'll be back in the lobby in ten minutes."

As Steve nodded and walked away, Jacob looked back at Ariel. "What were you saying?" he asked.

"Nothing," said Ariel. "Nothing."

Chapter Fifteen

As she listened to the ring on the other end of the line, Ariel rubbed her eyes. They were smarting, burning. For what felt like the thousandth time in the past few days, she was on the verge of tears. She hadn't cried so much in years. Sure, she'd been on autopilot. Going through the motions of life. Focusing on her career, on external markers of success. Ignoring her emotions.

Jacob Hunter had changed her. Broken through her defenses. She *felt* again. It was like he had given her the gift of herself . . . access to a deep well of love and faith. Her heart was broken. But at least she knew it was there.

The phone rang on and on. Ariel bit her lip, tried to pull herself together. She was dreading the moment when Theo answered. She knew he would. He was umbilically attached to his cell. She didn't want to say what she had to say. Didn't want to do what she knew she had to do.

Theo picked up. "Hi, sweetie!" he chirped.

Ariel choked back a sob. Theo would never understand everything that was at stake for her in this conversation. She just had to get through it. Make him believe that this wasn't the most heart-wrenching decision she'd ever made—that it was no big deal.

Hadn't Theo himself said she was a good actress?

Aiming for a casual tone, Ariel replied: "Hi, boss. How're things in the big city?"

"There's nothing new under the sun, my dear," Theo answered, chuckling. Then the question Ariel dreaded: "How're things with you? How's the story coming along? Have you dug deep? Do you have tantalizing details to share with me and your reading public?"

"Theo," Ariel took a deep breath, "I can't write the story. I'm so sorry. I'm sorry to have wasted your time. The magazine's money. I feel terrible."

"Ariel," Theo asked testily, "why on earth can't you write the story? *A* story? *Any* story? Even if Jacob Hunter isn't using drugs, he's an interesting character. I'm sure you can come up with something worthwhile to say about him. You're an excellent, incisive journalist. You have a fascinating subject. Make something out of it."

"I can't explain to you why I can't write the story," Ariel whispered. "Any story. You're going to have to take my word for it. I know that's a huge leap of faith and that I haven't done anything this past week to merit that kind of trust. But I hope you can trust me." She paused. "I haven't found out anything interesting about Jacob Hunter at all." Ariel hated lying. But sometimes it had to be done.

There was a long pause on the other end of the line. When Theo spoke again, it was in a different tone. "Are you all right, Ariel? You know I don't care about the story as much as I care about you. I hope you'd tell me if there was anything wrong."

Ariel shook her head, squeezing her eyes shut against the tears that wanted to come. She was *so* not all right. Then she realized that Theo couldn't see her shaking her head from New York City.

Verbalize, Ariel, she told herself. *You do this all the time.*

"I'm fine," she told Theo, then repeated herself in a more confident tone of voice: "I'm fine. Thank you for asking. I miss you. I miss the city. I want to come home." Another lie.

She wondered, for the thousandth time, if she was doing the right thing. No matter how much she loved him—and she did love him, tremendously, passionately—she couldn't see how a relationship between her and Jacob Hunter could possibly work out.

He was an international cycling star who spent most of the year traveling from place to place, training from dawn to dusk, in the company of his teammates. If she tried to go with him, she'd be nothing but a camp follower. A groupie. She couldn't see herself in that role. And she couldn't imagine asking Jacob to give up his cycling career for her, even to step it down, to stay in the same place for part of the year, every year. Cycling was what he lived for. The thing he loved more than her.

He might agree to it. Might settle down with her, and be happy, for a few years. But he would grow to resent it. When he felt himself, year after year, falling short of his potential. Competing at less than full capacity. When the thrill of their relationship had faded, their passion had cooled—as it inevitably would—he'd resent *her*.

She couldn't stand to think that Jacob would one day hate her. She wouldn't make him choose. Wouldn't let him be torn between two loves.

She was leaving. While it was still possible. For Jacob. For herself. It was the hardest thing she'd ever done.

"Theo," she said, "I need to come home as soon as possible. I feel disappointed in myself. Homesick. Please get me on a flight as quick as you can."

Theo paused again before speaking. She knew she wasn't fooling him entirely. He could tell something was wrong. He knew her too well to buy her "homesick" act.

The biggest lie she'd told hadn't been about the story. It was when she'd called New York City "home." Right now, no place that didn't have Jacob in it could possibly feel like home.

But she had to trust that that would change. That her heart would repair itself. That she could submerge herself in her old life, and that eventually it would feel right again. She would try to hold on to the healing power of love, even though it would hurt. Even though it would take a long, long time before she could sleep through the night without waking up. Without her body aching for his warmth. His touch.

"Ariel," Theo said gently, "I'll see if there are any flights later today. I'll email you the itinerary. Take care of yourself, all right?"

"Thank you," Ariel whispered. When she hung up the phone, she was shaking like a leaf. Quaking like an aspen. She was tough. She was resilient. But she couldn't imagine recovering from this one.

Ariel stayed in her room. She got an email from Theo almost immediately. He'd managed to get her on an early afternoon flight. She packed and waited until it was time to leave. She wanted to get this over with as quickly as possible.

Her cell phone rang several times. It was Jacob. Ariel didn't answer. Then the room phone rang. Ariel figured he'd changed his strategy. She didn't answer those calls, either.

A little before noon, Ariel called down to the desk to request that her car be brought up from the garage. She wanted to spend as little time in the lobby as possible. Less chance of running into Jacob.

She smiled a humorless smile. Ironic that the person she most wanted to see was also the person she needed to avoid at all costs. She left the room and wheeled her suitcase down the hall. She couldn't help feeling like she was sneaking out, tail between her legs. Making an undignified escape.

When she got down to the lobby she kept her head down and walked toward the doors as quickly as possible. She looked up only when she was three quarters of the way to the exit and was utterly horrified to see, idling behind her coupe, Jacob's team RV, with several of his teammates lounging on the curb. Before she had a moment to process what she'd seen, to figure out what to do—other than run in the opposite direction—she heard what she most dreaded hearing. Jacob was behind her, calling her name. With a horrible, sick feeling in her stomach, she turned to face him.

"Ariel!" he called. His face was shining, his eyes glowing. He was filled with excitement—to see her. He was wearing his kit; all the contours of the body she loved were gorgeously displayed. Ariel's heart was already broken. Now it exploded into dust.

Jacob approached. She could see the light in his eyes dim, his steps slow, as he registered her dejected demeanor. Her pained expression. He reached out to embrace her, then dropped his arms when he saw her flinch away from his touch. Ariel knew that if he touched her, she'd be lost.

"Ariel," Jacob said, a frown of concern furrowing his brow, "what's the matter? Are you all right?"

The same question Theo had asked her. *No*, she wanted to scream, *I am* not *all right!* Before she had a chance to reply, Jacob's eyes dropped to the suitcase at her feet. His expression changed—to one of shock. Of horror.

"Are you leaving?" he asked her in a tone of utter incredulity.

"Yes," said Ariel, as calmly as she could. "Something's come up. I have to go back to New York immediately."

"Were you planning to tell me this?" Jacob asked, frowning. "I've been trying to get a hold of you all day."

"I'm sorry, Jacob. It's all been very sudden."

"Well, are you coming back?" Jacob asked. He looked uncomfortable. Ariel could practically see the gears turning in his head. All the logistical problems that made their relationship impossible were occurring to him for the first time. The problems she'd been torturing herself over all morning.

"No, Jacob." Ariel shook her head. "You know I can't. My life is in New York. Yours is, well . . . everywhere. This can't work. If you think about it, you'll see I'm right. I'm so sorry. I hope you'll remember me kindly." The stiff, awkward phrasing was repellent to her. She smiled what had to be a tight, sickening smile. Before she had a chance to break, to collapse into his arms, she turned and walked away from him. Her heart was brimming over—with love stronger than anything she'd ever felt, with sadness poignant and overwhelming. She knew she'd remember the look on his face for the rest of his life.

*

Jacob stood and watched her go. His mind refused to process what she'd just told him. He knew it was important. That he needed to understand it. *Think, Hunter*, he told himself. But the feeling of shock, of suspension, was too strong.

Only the absolute horror he felt when he saw Ariel step into her car and drive away jolted him into action. *I don't need to understand,* he thought as he sprinted toward the RV, *I just need to get her back.*

His teammates scattered in surprise as he bolted through the door. He dragged the mountain bike that Randall had stashed inside out onto the pavement, launched himself onto the seat, clicked into the pedals, and sprinted after her as fast as he'd ever done at the end of a race.

Steven and Randall ran behind him, yelling, "Jacob! No!" He knew why they wanted him to stop. He wasn't even wearing a helmet. He was riding like a maniac, weaving madly between cars. The Colorado Classic was in two days. By jeopardizing himself, he was jeopardizing the success of the whole team. All their training. Blood, sweat, and tears. Jacob was poised to win the classic; the rest of the team was poised to support him. They were all in the best condition of their lives. At the peak of their fitness. They'd all worked incredibly hard to get there.

And it could all change, very quickly, if Jacob kept riding the way he was riding at that moment.

Jacob couldn't care less. Nothing—even the race that, two weeks ago, he would have given several years of his life to win, nor the teammates he'd been through so much with—mattered more than finding Ariel. Than stopping her.

He turned off the main street onto smaller side streets, then onto dirt roads leading up into the hills. He wasn't going to catch Ariel by following her down the highway. Finally, he turned off the road entirely, onto a winding trail that clung hazardously to the sides of precipices and plunged through rocky, punishing terrain—only to rise again, steeply and suddenly.

Jacob had never been so grateful for the effects of his years of training, the payoff for his superhuman efforts. The strength, the conditioning, the handling skills that allowed him to hurl himself fearlessly over and through rock outcroppings, treacherously twisted roots, sharp dips and bumps that sent him flying through the air. He never stopped pedaling. He was pushing himself harder than he'd ever pushed himself before. It was the last thing he should be doing two days before an important—potentially life-changing—race.

But if he lost Ariel, he would lose more than a race. Cyclist's hearts could grow in their chests throughout years of training, could beat harder and faster than any other athlete's. Without Ariel, none of it would matter. His heart was the most developed muscle in his body. But if he lost Ariel, it would stop. There would be no reason for it to continue beating.

He reached the ridge of the last hill between him and the curving highway. He'd ridden the most direct route between two points. The road had gone around a mountain—he'd gone over it. His only hope was to cut Ariel off on the stretch of pavement directly below him.

He saw the red coupe round the bend that would carry her past him—and away. Setting the bike directly downhill—bypassing the switch-back trails that would have led him more safely down the precipitous mountainside—sliding through shale and scree, Jacob plummeted through space, his wheels barely in contact with the dangerously uneven ground.

Now he was risking not just his training, his team, his race—but his life. At the last moment, Jacob burst onto the pavement, breaking hard and whirling to face the red coupe as it sped directly toward him.

*

Ariel almost couldn't stop in time. She squealed to a halt, brakes smoking, heart pounding with the sudden shock of adrenaline. She didn't realize for a moment that the figure in front of her—facing down the car like a matador facing a dangerous bull—was Jacob.

Shaking, she pulled the coupe to the side of the highway—and toppled out directly into Jacob's arms. He kissed her hair, her head, her face—then her lips. Urgently. Passionately. She pulled away.

"You're a lunatic," she gasped. "I could have killed you." Her heart quailed at the thought. She was still shaking. With fear. With relief. With love.

"Okay, I'm a lunatic," Jacob panted, cupping her face in her hands. "But remember, what's the most important thing about me?"

Ariel's laugh was choked. "You're fast," she said weakly. She tried to turn her head and he released her. She looked up at the shockingly steep slope he'd ridden down. Shuddered.

"Wrong," he said. "I *am* fast." He grinned his cocksure grin. "The fastest. But the most important thing about me . . . " He took a deep breath.

"The most important thing about me," he began again. "Is that . . . I love you." The grin returned, less cocksure. Was Jacob Hunter nervous?

Ariel wasn't going to keep him in suspense. She kissed him. He kissed her back with equal fervor. She couldn't believe the relief she'd felt. That he'd stopped her. Hadn't let her leave. That she hadn't lost him after all.

"But *cycling* is your life," said Ariel. She didn't leave the circle of his arms, just pulled back far enough to look him in the eyes. "You're a genius on the bike. It's your calling. I don't want to get in the way of that. And I don't know how your calling, and *my* calling, won't get in the way of us."

"I don't know, either," said Jacob. "It'll be a challenge." He grinned. "We both like challenges."

"*You* like challenges," said Ariel.

Jacob's grin widened. "You *are* a challenge," he said. "Ariel, the logistics will be tricky. I can't deny that. But those are details. This . . . " He kissed her. "*This*, this thing between the two of us, this isn't a detail."

"It's the real deal, huh, Hunter?" asked Ariel, the light starting to shine in her eyes.

"The real deal," he said.

She buried her hands in his hair, pulling his head down to her, his lips to her lips. He caressed her breasts, her hips, every luscious curve, crushing her against him with all his strength. His hands were so rough. It should have hurt. But nothing had ever felt so right. So much like a homecoming.

Ariel realized she wasn't breathing.

She rested her head against his chest, trying to catch her breath, and he held her, tightly but more gently, his lips resting on the top of her head. She was stunned, intoxicated.

"Jacob," Ariel whispered, "if you don't want to make love to me on the side of the highway, you'd better get me back to the hotel, ASAP."

"Who says I don't want to make love to you on the side of the highway? It's pretty romantic, as highways go." Jacob's voice was thoughtful. "Ground is rocky, I'll admit."

"I'd mention the potential dangers . . . sheer drops, oncoming cars . . . but after the stunt you just pulled I think 'danger' doesn't register with you." She followed this up with a muffled expletive that sounded like, "something-something knucklehead."

Jacob laughed, and Ariel heard it rumbling deep in his chest. She pressed closer to him, held him so that his heart thudded against her ear. His heartbeat reverberated through every part of her body. *It could beat for both of us,* she thought, snuggling against his chest, kissing his collarbone, his throat.

"So what were you saying about making love on the side of the highway?" Jacob asked, weaving his hands through her hair and tugging her head back, locking her eyes with his, burning her with the golden flame kindled in their depths.

Ariel arched an eyebrow. Glanced at the gravel shoulder of the road where it gave way to wildflowers.

"I might have to think about this one," she said.

"Let's think later," Jacob suggested.

"That's what I meant," said Ariel, and with a grin that rivaled his own, she pulled him down into the bank of columbines.

Epilogue

The door to Karen's room opened at Beth's gentle knock—the bright-eyed girl within rocketed through the doorway and threw herself into her mother's arms.

"Mom!" she exclaimed. "I couldn't sleep, I'm so excited. Is this shirt too much? Will I embarrass Jakey?"

She was wearing a t-shirt in team colors that showed Jacob riding his bike in profile. It read "Hunter" across the back. The thick material of the t-shirt made a tent on her skinny frame in a way that wasn't strictly flattering, but the animated expression on her wan face made all the difference. She looked beautiful.

"Where did you get that?" marveled Beth Hunter.

"The Internet," said Karen simply.

"Of course." Beth smiled. "I don't think Jake will be embarrassed. I already signed you out with Bettina. Are you ready to go?"

"Ready!" chirped Karen. Then more seriously, "I'm so grateful to you for arranging this. For talking to Bettina and getting permission for me to miss groups. I've never gotten to see Jakey race in person before! Well, maybe I did once. Some race when we were kids. But it was really boring and I don't think I actually saw anything."

"Well, you know we won't be seeing this whole race either," Beth said. "Just the end."

"That's all that matters, right?" Karen giggled. "The part where Jake blows everyone else away?"

Beth answered Karen's bright smile with one of her own.

Karen's eyes shifted to Ariel, who was hanging shyly behind Beth. Beth followed her daughter's gaze, and leaned close to Karen's ear. "Yep, that's her," she told her, "that's Ariel. She is, as my mother would say, the genuine article."

Karen grinned and with no warning launched herself at Ariel, who hesitated only a moment before returning her tight hug.

"I'm so glad to meet you," both women said simultaneously, then looked at each other and broke into laughter. Chattering comfortably— like they'd known each other forever—they left the hospital together and climbed into Beth's Subaru. The car was a present from Jacob.

"I wanted to get you something small and zippy," he'd said. "Like a Porsche. But the guy at the dealership told me these handle better in the snow." The Hunters now always referred to the Subaru as "The Porsche." Ariel found the habit endearing.

"Hold onto your hats, girls," said Beth as she squealed out of her parking spot. "The engine's in the back."

Richard was waiting for them on the square of sidewalk they'd staked out for themselves directly in front of the finish line.

"Don't worry, you didn't miss anything," he said. "I haven't seen a thing." Ariel stiffened, expecting to see bitterness on Richard Hunter's handsome, lined face, but she relaxed when she saw that he was smiling with genuine good humor.

Beth gave a surprised laugh. Linking her husband's arm with her own, she rested her head affectionately against his shoulder.

"Honey," she said, as though scandalized. "That sounded suspiciously like a joke." Then she gave Ariel a conspiratorial grin, a grin that somehow seemed to say thank you. Ariel smiled, even though she didn't feel that she deserved the gratitude she saw in Beth's eyes. She couldn't take the credit for Richard Hunter's new attitude. He was fighting his own demons, and she couldn't begin to imagine the courage it took to walk out in these pushing, shoving crowds, the courage it took to rely on his wife, and on her, a young woman he barely knew, for help. But she was happy that the whole family had taken her so immediately into the warm circle of support and love they created between them.

"We're all here," Beth said. "It'll mean so much to Jacob . . . whether he wins or loses."

Ariel, looking at them dreamily—father, mother, and daughter—felt jolted. She realized for the first time that she'd never really thought about what would happen if Jacob lost. As soon as the idea occurred to her, however, she dismissed it. It wasn't that she didn't think it was possible. Jacob had given her a crash course in bike racing in the last few days—"crash" being the operative word. Ariel shuddered when she thought of Jacob being involved in the kinds of collisions he'd shown her in videos of famous races. With all her heart, she wanted him to get through the race in one piece.

Assuming that he did, though, she couldn't care less whether he won or lost. When she'd first met him, she'd thought he was an egomaniac, an immature, self-absorbed star who cared only about winning, and who would probably have a tantrum if he didn't.

Now that she knew him better, Ariel understood that Jacob was made of stronger stuff. His apprenticeship in the rough-and-tumble world of European cycling had schooled him in the dangers of over-confidence. He'd suffered his share of defeats, and he always bounced back, ready for more. He was both humble and relentless. He understood that sometimes a win was impossible, but that this was never a reason to give less than his all.

Standing at the finish line, Ariel craned her neck to see if the cyclists were coming into view. She knew it was too soon. Knew that the crowd stretching down both sides of the road would alert her to their approach. But she couldn't help it. Her heart was pounding with vicarious excitement, the amped-up feeling of the waiting crowd.

As she waited, she realized that she was obsessively fingering the charms on her bracelet. She looked down and smiled. She was holding the tiny gold bicycle Jacob had given her as though it were a good luck charm. She had no idea where he'd found it. When he'd given her the small jeweler's box over dinner the night before, she hadn't known what to expect. She already knew she wanted to marry him. But she hadn't expected it to happen so fast. She stared down at the box. As if reading her mind, Jacob lifted her chin, and shot her one of his trademark heart-stopping grins.

"We both know I'm fast," he laughed. "But it's not magic. I worked for it. And I'm going to work to win you for my wife. And I know that will take a little more time."

Half disappointed and half relieved, Ariel opened the box . . . and crowed with delight.

"It's beautiful!" she exclaimed. "Perfect!" How could she explain to him that the charm meant more to her than a ring would have? It meant he knew her more deeply than she could ever have hoped for. Understood, at a gut level, what mattered to her the most.

She wished Jacob could have known her father. She wished her father could have known her Jacob.

They would have talked about Shakespeare, she thought. *They would have gone fishing in the Hudson. My father would have come out here and seen Colorado. He would have loved it. The mountains. The rivers. We would have walked through fields of columbines and I wouldn't have been able to keep myself from dancing.*

The ache would never go away. But somehow loving Jacob made it easier. She had learned about love from her father and mother, and every minute with Jacob reminded her. Sweetly.

Not knowing what words could possibly suffice to express her gratitude, Ariel had risen from her chair, rounded the table, and plopped herself down in his lap, her arms around his neck. She'd kissed him deeply, right in the middle of the restaurant. Within thirty seconds, he was asking for the check.

Behind her, Karen and her father were having a tentative but heartfelt reunion. Beth was standing back, giving them space to talk with one another. Ariel was also trying to give them their privacy, but it was hard, on a cramped sidewalk with people pressing in from all sides, and occasional snatches of their conversation drifted up to her.

" . . . describe everything," Karen was saying, "so you won't miss a single detail. You'd never believe my t-shirt. It's Jakey on his bike with a maroon background and . . . "

Then later, Richard's huskier voice: "Karen, I want to apologize . . . inexcusable not to visit . . . love you so much."

When Ariel looked back, they were embracing one another, and there were tears in Karen's eyes and in Richard Hunter's blind ones as well.

A gasp traveled through the crowd. From farther down the road, Ariel heard cheering, progressing toward her in a roaring crescendo. The leading group was not yet in sight. But she could hear the spectators further down shouting the names of their favorite riders . . . Ariel thought she could pick out the sound of fans chanting "Hunter! Hunter! Hunter!" She was so excited, she wanted to jump up and down.

When the leaders came into sight, she couldn't hold herself back. She jumped, pumped her fists in the air and screamed Jacob's name— even before she realized that he was leading the breakaway, Randall and Steven close behind him. They were riding in a tight pack, several lengths ahead of any of the other riders. Gearing up for the sprint, they stood up on their pedals and leaned forward, beginning to pump their legs faster and faster, muscles bulging from their thighs and their forearms. Their clenched jaws and furrowed brows communicated the superhuman effort they were putting forth.

The line separated as the riders put everything they had into the last hundred yards of road leading up to the finish line. Jacob drew ahead of his teammates, pedaling furiously, a look of pure, intense focus on his chiseled features. Ariel was screaming his name at the top of her lungs, jumping again and again into the air, urging him on with her voice, her body, all of her will.

Jacob swept over the finish line, several seconds ahead of the next rider. As he crossed the line, he sat up in his seat and raised his arms—V for victory—with a look of the purest, simplest happiness on his gorgeous face. Ariel couldn't help it. She burst into tears.

Behind her, she heard Beth, Karen, and Richard yelling Jacob's name. As the rest of the riders, followed by the support vehicles, came over the line, the crowd broke apart, milling into the street toward the stage and the podium.

Ariel couldn't see Jacob anymore. Leaving his family, she pushed through the crowd to find him. He was standing beside his bike, near the stage, sluicing himself down with water from a squirt bottle. He was still breathing hard, covered in sweat. He'd unzipped his skinsuit and pulled the top down to his waist, revealing the contours of his gleaming, golden torso, his broad shoulders and taut abdomen. Ariel gasped as a wave of desire, incredibly strong, swept through her.

She was running to him. He raised his eyes and saw her, and his smile grew even wider. Disregarding his disheveled state, Ariel threw herself into his arms. Jacob lifted her from the ground, supporting her whole body against him. She kissed his forehead, his cheek, his chin. His skin was hot. He tasted salty. She wanted more of it, more of him. She found his lips, kissed him hungrily. Jacob's chest was heaving with the incredible exertion of the race and she knew she should let go of him, let him catch his breath, but when she tried to pull back, he held her. He deepened the kiss, sweeping Ariel's mouth with his tongue. She moaned into his mouth, nipping playfully at his lower lip. The sound of clapping arose around them. Bemused, Jacob lowered Ariel to the ground and they looked around to see Jacob's teammates, grinning and applauding.

That might have been the happiest moment of Ariel's life. Or it might have been when she stood with his family below the stage, watching Jacob on the top step of the podium, receiving his medal. He dedicated his win to Karen. Ariel didn't mind at all. She wanted, more than anything, for Karen to know how much her brother loved her.

Ariel already knew. She was completely, unshakably, irrevocably certain that Jacob Hunter loved her.

Just the way she loved him.

"What about this Fratello?" Theo had asked during their last conversation. "Is he on drugs? Or Henderson? Anyone on the team? Someone has to be on drugs."

"Nope." Ariel had laughed. "How about I write you an article about the power of avocadoes?"

"Genetically modified avocadoes?" Theo sounded perkier. "I've been wanting to run some kind of Frankenfood piece . . . maybe we can get in on the soy controversy? I'll have to think about this one. We'll talk when you're back in New York."

"We'll probably talk before I'm back in New York," Ariel had laughed.

"Exactly," said Theo, and once she heard him begin to order his coffee, she hung up. She still had a job. That was good. Theo had actually screamed "Hallelujah!" when she'd told him about her and Jacob. "I couldn't think of any other reason you wouldn't write the story," he'd crowed. "I knew it had to be love. Or Rocky Mountain spotted fever. To be honest, I thought there was a fifty-fifty chance." Then the background noises had faded out. Theo had stopped multitasking. His voice had come through the phone crystal clear as he said, with unmistakable sincerity, "You made the right choice. Ariel, you deserve this."

Maybe someday she'd even be able to write the real story behind her abandoned article on Jacob Hunter. It turned out to be a little light on the drugs. But there was sex. A *lot* of sex. She grinned. Sometimes sex isn't just sex . . . it's trust. It's true love. What would all the cynical New Yorkers think about that scoop?

They'd think it was incredible. Sensational. They wouldn't know whether or not to believe it. Even her friend Jenna, champion of romantic serendipity, had barely believed it when she'd called to give her the good news.

Believe it. That was the moral, thought Ariel. Every now and then, something seems too good to be true. And it is.

It's better.

About the Author

Toni Jones grew up in Wyoming, Utah, and Colorado, and she continues to appreciate the special beauty and unique lifestyle of the Western U.S. Her passion for the outdoors and her love of romance go hand-in-hand. She hopes her work will inspire all her readers to get outside and fall in love under the open sky!

In the mood for more Crimson Romance? Check out *Catch of the Year* by Brenda Hammond at *CrimsonRomance.com*.